"I'm sure you know more than you're letting on...

"I'm going to figure out what you're doing here and I'm going to expose you."

Jeez. Everything sounded sexual when he was standing this close. She upped the ante and took a half step closer to him. She definitely wasn't going to let him intimidate her in this sexy game of cat and mouse.

"You can try, but there's nothing to expose. What you see is what you get."

"Oh, I very much doubt that, Ms. Evans. The truth is hiding somewhere behind that big hair and tiny suit."

"Look at me, Mr. Maguire. You honestly think there's room to hide anything under this?"

Her breath stuttered at the sudden fierceness in his eyes, the predatory gleam that pinned her in place. Were their lips getting closer because he was leaning in, or had she swayed toward him?

She was drawn to his body, hard as iron and just as magnetic. Her fingers brushed his biceps as his hands made first contact with her waist and his lips moved closer, then closer still...

Dear Reader,

I usually don't remember how ideas get from my brain to the page, but this novel's origin story can be traced back to a cold, snowy evening while watching *Hockey Night in Canada*. (What? A Canadian who likes hockey? It's true. I'm also a woman with way too many pairs of shoes. Embracing clichés is good for the soul, eh?)

At one point in the game, the TV announcer was talking about a defenseman and actually said, I kid you not, "He's a big, strong farm boy with good hands."

Um...yes please! I'll take one of those.

And the Women's Hockey Network was born. My friend and I joked endlessly about *Sexy Sports Coverage for Her*, complete with play-off beard analysis ("As you can see from this graph, peak attractiveness was reached here, when he was sporting six days' worth of stubble in game three of the first series."), and some risqué, double-entendre commentating ("I really admire the way he keeps such a firm grip on his stick. That kind of control is going to result in some great scoring opportunities.").

Our inside joke was a romance novel waiting to happen, and Luke and Holly were the perfect duo for the job. They're both incredibly career-focused, and it was a blast to bodycheck them out of their comfort zones and into each other's arms.

By the way, do you like the internet? I hang out there sometimes at tarynleightaylor.com, facebook.com/tarynltaylor1 and on Twitter @tarynltaylor. You should totally swing by if you're in the neighborhood.

Keep on dreaming out loud,

Taryn Leigh Taylor

Taryn Leigh Taylor

Playing to Win

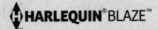

Recycling programs
for this product may
not exist in your area.

ISBN-13: 978-0-373-79882-7

Playing to Win

Copyright © 2016 by Taryn Leigh Taylor

This edition published by arrangement with Harlequin Books S.A.

For questions and comments about the quality of this book, please contact us at CustomerService@Harlequin.com.

® and TM are trademarks of Harlequin Enterprises Limited or its corporate affiliates. Trademarks indicated with ® are registered in the United States Patent and Trademark Office, the Canadian Intellectual Property Office and in other countries.

Printed in U.S.A.   www.Harlequin.com

Taryn Leigh Taylor likes dinosaurs, bridges and space, both personal and of the final-frontier variety. She shamelessly indulges in clichés, most notably her Starbucks addiction (grande six-pump whole-milk no-water chai tea latte, aka: the usual), her shoe hoard (I can stop anytime I... Ooh! These are pretty!) and her penchant for falling in lust with fictional men with great abs. She also really loves books, which is what sent her down the crazy path of writing one in the first place.

Want to be virtual friends? Check out tarynleightaylor.com, facebook.com/tarynleightaylor1 and twitter.com/tarynltaylor.

Books by Taryn Leigh Taylor

Harlequin Blaze

Kiss and Makeup

This one's for my Women's Hockey Network cohost, and the best amanuensis in the business. Cool Crystal, I owe you a slab of cake with a cupcake on top.

To Adrienne, who always makes my stories better. I don't have the words to thank you enough. (But editors like irony, right?)

My love forever to Uncle Don and Auntie Shirl for keeping it real and staying true to the home team amidst a sea of red.

Mimsy, Dadoo and the man behind Grammataco— I'm so lucky to have you guys in my corner. High fives and secret handshakes all around.

And to my Palisades Crew: Michele, Michelle, Lori, Carolyne, Marilyn and Laura. The kind of women, and writers, who inspire me even now.

1

"QUIT SQUIRMING, HOL. You look totally porn-hot."

Holly Evans glared at her friend and cameraman. "Well, thanks, Jay. I feel so much better now. After all, 'porn-hot' is just what we professional sportscasters aspire to, right, Corey?"

She immediately regretted throwing the question to the reporter setting up a few feet down the rubber-floored hallway. Corey Baniuk was Portland's favorite on-the-scene sports authority...at least for now.

Rumor had it that Jim Purcell, the longtime sports anchor at *Portland News Now*, was contemplating retirement and that Corey had a lock on the in-studio position. That meant Holly's dream job might soon be up for grabs—and Holly intended to do the grabbing. Provided she hadn't screwed up all her credibility by playing Sports Reporter Barbie for the next three months, of course.

"Sure." Corey shot her the familiar, good-natured grin that was a staple of both the six and eleven o'clock news. "Someone will be by to oil my chest any minute."

His camera guy chuckled and heat prickled up Holly's

cheeks, no doubt rivaling the fire-engine-red color of her outfit. She forced a wan smile—small thanks for him taking the high road, but it was all she could muster. God, she envied him his conservative gray pinstripe suit. And he was even wearing a shirt under his jacket. She would give up her firstborn for a shirt.

"How did this happen?" she lamented in Jay Buchanan's general direction. "I am an intelligent, educated woman who is passionate about all things sports." She glanced down at her brazen skirt suit, but with her boobs pushed up to her chin, not much of it was visible to her.

Damn Victoria and all her secrets.

"When did I become the Hooters girl of broadcasting?"

Jay rolled his eyes. "Hey, you knew what you were signing up for. Hell, I'll bet Lougheed had dollar signs circling his head when he saw your audition tape."

Holly cringed at her friend's choice of words. "It wasn't an audition tape," she protested weakly. "It was a favor for you. And a fight against injustice."

When she'd agreed to shoot the joke video with Jay's fledgling production company, she was aiming for satire, intending it to be biting commentary on how female sports reporters were perceived. It was an attempt to show people the stereotypes she fought against every day in pursuit of her dream. Instead, she was now the star of a bona fide viral video, sporting a teased-out helmet of blond hair and freezing her butt off while she pretended to be hockey-impaired.

It had caught the attention of Ron Lougheed, the GM of Portland's professional hockey team, and the ditzy routine was now, sadly, the best on-camera experience she'd been offered since she'd graduated broad-casting school.

"No one cares what it *was*. What the Women's Hockey Network *is*, is a YouTube sensation! People are eating it up and coming back for seconds. To the suits, you're the living, breathing, high-heel-wearing crowbar they're gonna use to pry into the coveted female demographic."

"And they somehow figure short skirts are going to help me accomplish that lofty goal?" she asked snidely, tugging said skirt back down her thighs.

"Hell, no! That's to keep the guys interested while you're talking about girly stuff like player hairdos."

With a deep breath of arena—rubber and concrete and sweat and ice—Holly called upon the stupid yoga class she'd suffered through two years ago at her best friend Paige's behest. Something about a mind/body connection, and inner peace, and deep breaths, and— ah, screw it.

Time to suck it up, Princess.

Jay was right. She'd accepted the job as the Portland Storm's web reporter for the duration of their play-off run, and if dressing like someone's too-slutty-to-acknowledge cousin was the price of breaking into her dream career, then that's what she'd do. She gave a determined nod at the thought, slamming a mental door on the last remnants of her doubt.

The buzzer sounded to hail the end of the game, and Holly's newly minted courage took a nosedive. This was it. Her debut.

She watched with mounting nerves as twenty massive men in skates and full equipment stalked toward her.

And speaking of porn-hot...

There he was: Luke Maguire, team captain, number eighteen, a premier left-winger with a career-best thirty-seven goals in the regular season this year. Not to mention sexy as hell and in possession of all of his teeth—no rare feat after six years in professional hockey. The man looked incredible, all tall and sweaty and pissed off over the loss of their first play-off game against Colorado.

When she caught his eye, she was torn somewhere between lust and duty. Then his gaze dropped to the straining top button of her suit jacket, and she felt extreme mortification enter the mix. He slowed his pace, lifted his beautiful blue eyes from her cleavage to her face and stepped out of the single-file line of burly hockey players to take a question. *From her.*

This was it. Her big moment. Thirty seconds with one of the elite players of the game. But instead of being able to ask something pertinent, like his thoughts on the lackluster performance of the Storm's players, or his musings on the unprecedented twenty penalty minutes they'd accrued, she was contractually obligated to say:

"This is Holly Evans of the Women's Hockey Network, and with me tonight is the captain of the Portland Storm, Luke Maguire! Luke, it's play-off season, a time when superstitions run rampant and hockey players all over the league stop shaving, even though a recent study shows that women prefer the clean-shaven look to a full beard by a margin of almost four to one. Do you think tonight's loss had anything to do with the fact that you chose to shave today, and do you plan on reconsidering your stance on facial hair as the play-offs progress?"

One straight, brown eyebrow crooked up, the only indication he'd even heard her "question." (She was willing to concede that she was using the term loosely.)

Then he grabbed the logoed towel some *Sports Nation* lackey had slung on his shoulder, wiped the sweat from his face and turned and walked away.

"BUCK UP, CAP. Why so down?"

Luke took a deep breath and started pulling off the tape wound around his socks and shin pads. "You mean aside from getting shut out in our own building, setting a franchise record in penalty minutes and the looming press conference I have to spend assuring reporters that we know we sucked out there?"

As far as Luke was concerned, the only upside to their spectacular 5–0 loss to Colorado was that Coach Taggert had been so pissed that he'd refused post-game media access to the dressing room. At least they could shower, change and lick their wounds in relative peace.

Brett Sillinger, the Storm's eighth-round draft pick, ran a hand through his sweaty curls. "Well, sure. When you put it that way. But look at the bright side! We're loaded, and women throw themselves at us! We've got the best goddamn job in the world, bar none. And we're in the play-offs, baby!"

Luke's stomach lurched. "Trust me, rookie, I know we're in the play-offs."

Did he ever. It was a pretty big deal to some very rich people in some very high places, people who were…*eager* to see the team perform well in the franchise's first run for the cup since joining the league five years ago. That fact had been made abundantly—and repeatedly—clear to him in the month since they'd clinched their play-off spot.

It was also Luke's first time in the play-offs since the worst night of his life. Three years had passed, but the wound was still as fresh as ever.

He shoved the nightmarish memory back into the mental penalty box where it belonged, barely aware he'd reached for his helmet until he caught himself brushing his thumb across the number ten sticker he'd placed inside it—a talisman to keep him focused. With a sigh, he reached up and set his helmet on the shelf above his head.

He was the team captain now, he reminded himself. He had a job to do and he couldn't afford to wallow in personal issues. You couldn't lead a team to victory if they didn't trust you to take care of business. And yet he didn't seem to be leading the team anywhere but to an early play-off exit. They all needed to get their heads out of their asses.

"We won't be in the play-offs for long if we keep playing like we just did. I know there are some nerves in the room. This franchise has never been in the play-offs before, and no one here has ever won a championship. None of that matters. We need to play our game, stay hungry and determined.

"And we can't get sidetracked by the increased media scrutiny. Especially now that even the non-sports media are hunting for stories and interviews. The blonde out there actually asked me if I thought we lost because I'm not growing a play-off beard."

The entire dressing room went silent as Luke untied his skate. He glanced around at his eerily quiet teammates. "What?"

"Well, we *did* lose…"

Luke's face twisted with disgust. "Are you kidding me? It's the first game! None of you even have beards yet. You guys really buy into this 'no shaving' bull?"

The rookie stroked his pitiful day's worth of stubble.

"All I know is that I'm in this to win this, and if sportin' a Grizzly Adams gets me closer to a championship, then I'm on it like STDs on a hooker."

"You realize that three out of four women hate beards, right?" Luke pulled his skate off, hating that he'd actually reduced himself to quoting stats from that reporter.

Sillinger got a philosophical look on his face. "Shave and you get laid for a night. Do what it takes to score a championship ring, and you'll be up to your balls in puck bunnies for the rest of your life. I mean, seriously, Mags. A woman with a body like that reporter's names me her 'hockey hottie of the month,' and I'll answer any stupid question she asks."

Luke paused in the act of loosening his other skate. "What are you talking about?"

"Are you serious?" Sillinger's surprise was obvious. "Holly Evans? The Women's Hockey Network?"

Luke gave a bewildered shrug.

"Dude, she's all over YouTube! She does this girly hockey-analysis show that's gone viral. And in it, she named *you* the hottest hockey player in the league. The top brass practically begged her to be our web reporter during the play-offs! Do you guys believe this? Hot Stuff here doesn't even know who Holly Evans is!"

The announcement set off a round of catcalls and ribbing. Luke turned to his linemate, Eric Jacobs. The stoic centerman gave a shrug of his big shoulders and shook his head. Luke was relieved he wasn't the only one out of the loop on this.

"Okay, okay." Luke waited for the dressing room to quiet. "Let's stay focused, guys. The game might be over, but we've still got work to do."

Work that involved hours of ripping apart the carcass

of the worst game they'd played all year. The assembled jackals—uh, *reporters*—were going to eat him alive, Luke thought soberly. He shed the rest of his equipment and headed for the showers.

But that was the price of the *C* on his jersey. The price of earning a living doing what he loved. Which was an honor and a privilege, considering some people never got that chance. And others had it stolen from them. Luke sighed.

At least the evisceration wouldn't have anything to do with beard statistics and superstitious nonsense. And yet somehow Luke sensed that Holly Evans was a bigger threat than all the other sports reporters combined...

2

"THE STORM ESSENTIALLY played an entire period short-handed, which, given the dismal play of your PK unit, definitely contributed to tonight's loss. Can you give us any insight as to what led to this unprecedented number of penalties for the Storm?"

Holly hit the pause button on last night's broadcast and whirled on the couch to face her best friend, Paige Hallett. "Did you hear that? That was my question. Corey Baniuk just asked Luke Maguire *my* question. And did the dumb jock walk away without a word? No. He stood there and answered it, the jerk!"

"You asked him that question and he ignored you?" Paige looked offended on her behalf.

"Well, no. I asked him if he thought he might grow a play-off beard—then he ignored me. But that's the question I *wanted* to ask him. That was a great question!"

Paige turned back to the magazine she was perusing. "I'll take your word for it. He lost me when he started talking about China. Besides, why would the Storm play a whole period shorthanded? Seems kind of counterproductive to me."

Holly sighed and set the remote on her coffee table. "They didn't play an actual period shorthanded, they got twenty penalty minutes, so over the course of the game, they essentially played a man short for the length of a period. And he didn't say Peking, he said *PK* unit. When a team gets a penalty, they put out their best penalty killers, their *penalty kill* unit."

"Oh. Well, why didn't he just say that?"

"He did! He *did* say that, and Luke Maguire answered him, because it was a relevant question asked by a serious sports reporter."

Paige shot her a sympathetic look. "*You're* a serious sports reporter."

"No, *I'm* a traitor to my gender. Last night I wore a tiny suit and high shoes and made a mockery of everything I love."

"Would you cut yourself some slack? Those were some seriously great shoes I picked out for you to wear. Besides, the only way you're truly a traitor to your gender is the complete lack of readable magazines in your house." Paige held up the *Sports Illustrated* she was flipping through as proof. "Seriously. If these guys weren't shirtless, I'd throw this across the room in protest. Oh, wow." A dreamy smile spread across Paige's pretty face. "Who is *that*? Come to momma."

Holly glanced over at the glossy, two-page spread featuring a certain hot, shirtless hockey player. His brown hair was the perfect length between shorn and shaggy, his blue eyes intense as ever. He was sitting in the dressing room, kitted out in hockey gear from the waist down—pants, socks and skates—and all muscle and beautiful bronzed skin from the waist up. Behind him, his last name and a big number 18 gleamed white against the navy of his Storm jersey.

"That's *Luke Maguire*. The topic of my diatribe for the last twenty minutes? The man currently paused on my television?" Holly gestured at his stupid handsome face in HD.

"Well, why didn't you tell me he was so yummy? I would have paid better attention." She glanced at the television, presumably for the first time since her arrival. "*Mmm*. Maybe you were right. I should watch more hockey."

Holly couldn't help but smile. She had been trying to open Paige up to the wonders of sports for the better part of a decade now. How had Holly not realized the best way to turn Paige on to sports was to *turn Paige on*? "You're incorrigible, you know that?"

Paige smiled sweetly. "I'm a divorcée with no serious relationship prospects on the horizon. I have to take my thrills where I can get them." She flicked her gaze back to the TV. "And that man looks like he gives good thrill."

Holly couldn't argue. Irrationally, it made her even angrier at him. At one of her favorite hockey players. One day of playing dress-up and her view of the sports world was already starting to become skewed. So far, a steady paycheck was the only thing she enjoyed about this gig. Especially after such a mortifying first night. She'd taken the job because it was her chance to get on camera. One step closer to her big dream of talking sports on TV. But now...

"I'm wondering if taking this job was a mistake," she confessed.

Since she'd graduated, she'd been plugging away,

ghostwriting sports pieces for a bunch of online sports blogs. Hockey, basketball, baseball, football, golf…you name it, she wrote it. Not that anyone knew, since all her painstaking work was credited to "staff writer." But it was the only way she could continue to write for enough outlets to make a living. She spent what little free time she had busting her butt trying to get one of her sports op-eds picked up.

That was the kind of writing she really loved—not spewing facts and stats and scores, but interpreting them, putting them in context, figuring out what was making a team successful, suggesting what they could do to become more so, having a go at dumb managerial decisions and underperforming athletes.

That sort of in-depth analysis was the key to getting where she really belonged—on television, just like her mom used to be. She wanted to read her pieces aloud, share them with people who loved sports as much as she did. Anyone could read a teleprompter; Holly wanted to make an impact.

"I mean, Jay and I made the Women's Hockey Network video as a joke. And now it's gotten me closer to my goal of being on camera than any article I've ever written." Holly looked down, picking at the red lacquer Paige had insisted on slicking over her stubby nails. "But instead of feeling great about that, I feel like I've sold out. I'm a joke. I mean, can you even imagine what my mom would think of all this?"

"Woah. Back up the pity bus. I will not let you go down the mom road. She loved you and she would want what's best for you. But Hols, even if your mom was still alive, what's best for you would be your choice, not hers."

Holly flopped onto the couch. "I know. But I still worry about letting her down. When I accepted this gig, I thought it was going to be a case of 'all publicity is good publicity.' Now I'm not so sure."

She ran her hands down her face. "Luke Maguire believes I'm a total idiot! How can I ever do an in-depth interview with him now? And I don't even get to travel with the team! That's how dumb the questions I ask are supposed to be. I'm not worth a seat on a chartered plane that's already been paid for."

Paige glanced up from a picture featuring a shirtless LA Laker. "Lighten up, would you? It's been one day. This job is a stepping-stone—one with over a hundred thousand hits on YouTube so far. You never know where this opportunity could take you. Besides, what do you think the rest of your former sports broadcasting class-mates are doing right now? Interviewing team mascots and reporting on who scored the most baskets in soc-cer games played by twelve-year-olds? I'll bet you're closer to a real gig than any of them." Paige shut the magazine and tossed it onto the coffee table. "You're working with a real hockey team, interviewing some of the best players in the game. And yeah, it's not per-fect, but it could be a hell of a lot worse. So to quote a good friend of mine—" Paige arched one perfectly winged eyebrow "—*suck it up, Princess.* Go out there and do the job."

Holly sighed. "I hate it when you're right."

"Then you must hate me all the time," her friend lamented with a grin. It faded after a moment. "Was that enough of a pep talk? Because I'll bail on my date and we can go out for a drink if you want to talk this out some more."

"Oh, right! You have a date." Holly shook her head. "I keep forgetting since you've been so secretive about this mystery man of yours."

"It's new. We're still feeling each other out. Once we start feeling each other *up*, then I'll have some details to share." Paige was the only person in the world Holly knew who could pull off a wink with such aplomb.

"Of that I have no doubt. Now go and have fun. Besides, I'm already in the middle of a sports-related crisis. There's no way I can muster the fortitude and patience it would take to teach you that you don't score baskets in soccer right now."

Paige laughed at the jab.

Holly squared her shoulders. "Like you said, I made this choice. I'm going to honor this contract. Maybe I can even convince them to let me do some real reporting. Wow 'em so they give me a chance to document the Storm's first time in the play-offs with the gravitas and seriousness that it deserves."

"That's the spirit! You show those men who's boss." The phone rang just as Paige stood to leave. "See? That's probably some titan of the hockey world, impressed with your journalistic integrity and calling to poach you for his own team."

"Who else could it be?" Holly agreed drolly. "Say hi to your date for me."

"No way. Get your own man, which I hope you do soon. You're in desperate need of some hunky distraction in your life," Paige advised, heading for the door. "At the very least, this job will be great for that."

Holly rolled her eyes in a silent goodbye as she grabbed the handset of her phone, recognizing Jay's number on call display. Paige didn't like him very much, but Holly and Jay had hit it off immediately in broadcasting school.

When the Storm offered to let her pick her own cameraman, she'd eagerly snatched Jay away from filming weddings and local stories. It was a relief not to have to fake sports stupidity with at least one person.

"Hey. The footage looks great." Embarrassing as it might be for her personally, she had to admit that Jay had edited her interviews with Luke and the rest of the team into a professional-looking comedic montage that could now be viewed by the world at portlandstorm.com.

"I'm glad you think so, because the boss man agrees."

"What?"

"That's why I'm calling. Check your texts."

"Or you could just tell me since we're, you know, *on the phone*," she pointed out.

"Okay, smart-ass. It seems your big-haired alter ego can do no wrong. Hits on the Storm's website have increased twenty percent since your interview was posted last night. Usually after a loss, website traffic goes down. They've decided to give us an extra assignment."

"Oh, God." Holly cringed. She couldn't help it. A twenty percent uptick? That did not bode well for Operation: Journalistic Integrity. She'd be stuck asking about favorite childhood breakfast cereals for the rest of her career while important stories, like Luke Maguire's scoring drought that had now entered its twelfth game, went unmentioned.

On the upside, at least the team captain was so annoyed with her about the play-off beard thing that she could focus her insipid questions on the rest of the players. "What do they want us to film?"

"Some fluffy pregame interviews with the guys, tomorrow after their morning skate. The brass plans to air them as teasers between periods to help drive up website traffic. We're starting with the big three, then we'll try to fit in as much of the rest of the team as we can manage."

The big three: goaltender Jean-Claude LaCroix, centerman Eric Jacobs, and, because sometimes life sucked with a vengeance, captain and left-winger Luke Maguire. Holly couldn't bring herself to speak through the impending sense of doom.

THWACK.

Luke's slap shot missed the net completely.

God—*thwack*—damn—*thwack*—mother—*thwack*—fuc—

"Mags!"

Luke looked up from the line of pucks he was systematically assaulting to see Jean-Claude LaCroix—J.C. to his teammates—standing in the players' box. He was dressed in a navy T-shirt that mimicked the Storm's home jersey, this year's standard issue for doing press.

With another muttered curse, Luke skated over to the bench.

"I just finished with the reporter, and Eric's in the hot seat right now. Someone can cover for you with her if you want to grab a shower, but to avoid the wrath of the higher-ups, I'd suggest you get a move on."

Luke pulled off one of his gloves so he could remove his helmet and set them both on the boards. "Yeah, I'll be there in a minute."

"You okay, man?"

He ran a hand over his sweaty hair. "Sure. What could be wrong?"

J.C. gave him a look. "You're the one who snapped two sticks in practice and is still out here pounding the boards. You tell me."

Luke appreciated his friend's tact. It wasn't like his problem wasn't obvious.

He couldn't hit the net.

It had been twelve games since he'd scored a goal—the longest dry spell of his hockey career. But no matter how hard he practiced, how much extra time he logged out here working on his shot, when he was in the game, he froze up. And people were noticing. He'd read the grumblings in the paper, heard the callouts on television. Hell, people were even tweeting him to say he sucked. If he didn't get his act together soon, he'd be headed for some obligatory couch time with the sports psychologist. And that meant talking about Ethan, a fate he tried to avoid at all costs.

"It's nothing." Luke brushed it off, hoping his buddy would let it go.

J.C. shook his head, rejecting the lie. Luke should have known he would. They'd been playing hockey together on and off since they were fourteen years old. At this point, his goaltender could read him just as well off the ice as on.

"It's *not* nothing, man. Don't overthink it. Besides, scoring isn't the only way to help the team."

"Easy for you to say. Your save percentage was .916 this season. You're doing your part, but we won't win if we don't put pucks in the other guys' net." Luke's shoulders tightened under the weight of expectation—from management, the fans, his teammates... "I haven't scored in over a month. What am I supposed to do about that?"

"Just relax and play the game."

Luke rolled his eyes at the Zen advice. "This is the reason people hate goalies, you know? You're all a bunch of pretentious assholes."

J.C. just grinned. "I'll see you up there, okay?"

With a nod, Luke grabbed his helmet and glove and headed to the dressing room to shower and change, hoping he could clear his head before he faced Holly Evans. His brain conjured the memory of the curvy blonde in the siren-red outfit. Yet another complication he didn't need right now. Because last night, he'd done something stupid.

With a self-directed curse, he'd opened a new browser window and typed "The Women's Hockey Network" into the search field on YouTube.

And there she was, Holly Evans, all big blond hair and big brown eyes and big, beautiful breasts. In fact, she was damn near perfect...until she got to the Hockey Hunk of the Month segment.

He wanted to be pissed.

Instead, he was oddly flattered.

Sure, he wasn't wild about the fact she'd used that damned shirtless picture of him from last month's *Sports Illustrated*, but after his on-ice struggles over the last month, he found his battered self-esteem had sort of appreciated the boost from those pouty, shiny lips of hers.

She'd even managed to make the award about more than his pectorals, citing his work with his pet charity, Kids on Wheels, and explaining its focus on providing wheelchairs and wheelchair-friendly sports programs for kids in need. Hell, she'd even brought up his role as a goodwill ambassador for ice sledge hockey, a cause near and dear to his heart.

If he wasn't so firmly anti-reporter, he might have approved of the way she'd so beautifully shifted the focus from the nonsensical to something that actually mattered. But in the end, what mattered most was winning, and ogling the pretty reporter wasn't going to help him put the puck in the net.

Now, Luke stood outside the dressing room, temporarily set aside this morning so that she could make a mockery of the sport he loved, willing himself to man up and walk in.

He scratched his chin self-consciously, wishing to hell that he'd shaved this morning. He didn't want to give her the satisfaction of assuming his decision not to shave had anything to do with her. If he'd been given any kind of heads-up about being locked in a room with Little Miss Play-off Beard today, he definitely would've given a big middle finger to all the doubts she and his teammates had planted about their loss. But there'd been no warning until just before practice. No doubt about it, karma was a stone-cold bitch.

With a deep breath, he stepped through the door to find his linemate was just finishing up his interview.

"That was great, Eric." Holly's voice, warm and sexy, called to mind the drizzle of honey on cream. Luke subconsciously turned toward it.

God*damn*, the woman was gorgeous. She was rocking the painted-on suit again, but this time the color was the same teal as the stripes and the cresting wave on the Storm jersey. (A color which, according to the Women's Hockey Network color chart, indicated a driven personality whose inner turmoil was often masked by an outward appearance of calm.)

She was sporting mile-high heels, a barely there skirt, plenty of cleavage and that big, tousled hair that probably felt like a helmet of straw in real life, but always managed to look kinda sexy on TV. And yet, now that she wasn't just a caricature on his computer screen, but a living, breathing woman, smiling and putting the notoriously shy Eric Jacobs at ease as they finished up their interview, he found himself wondering what she'd look like in jeans and a T-shirt.

The thought irritated him. He just wanted to get this whole thing over with so he could concentrate on the important stuff. Like winning hockey games. He made himself take a step forward. "So I guess that means I'm up?"

With obvious relief, Jacobs flashed him a thankful smile, said a quick goodbye and fled the scene.

Holly whirled around, tugging at her skirt as though willing more fabric to appear. "Luke! Uh, Mr. Maguire, I—"

"Luke's fine."

They lapsed into an awkward silence.

She bit her lip.

Damn, her mouth is amazing. And he really needed to stop noticing that.

He pulled a frustrated hand down his face, cursing inwardly as he realized his mistake. Satisfaction sparked in those coffee-brown eyes of hers—he and his day's worth of stubble were busted. But to his surprise, her dawning smile was more teasing than mocking, and it made him want to wipe it off her face in a way that would be pleasurable for them both.

"You guys want to get started, or what?"

The cameraman's sudden intrusion jerked Luke out of a mental image in which he and Holly were long past "started" and well on their way to "finished."

What a hypocrite! He kept telling his guys to focus and here he was, distracted by a pretty face.

Except he sensed she was more than that. Something about her ditzy act wasn't quite right. There was more going on underneath the glossy surface she presented to the world, he just knew it. He trusted his instincts—his livelihood depended on them. His shot might be off, but his gut wasn't. And if Holly Evans had another agenda, she was a danger to him and his team. Then again, just the sight of her in that outfit was dangerous.

"What? Yes! Of course, Jay, thanks!" Holly's voice was about an octave too high and a six-pack of Red Bull too perky. She gave Jay an overly bright smile and snatched her interview cards from the stool. "Luke, if you'll take a seat?"

Like a good little soldier, Luke walked over and sat down.

"We'll start with a quick Q and A with just you on camera, and then I've got a couple of more in-depth questions that we'll shoot with the two of us on-screen."

"Yeah, sure." He tried to appear casual and nonchalant.

She gave Jay a nod and waited until the little red light on the camera flicked on and the boom was in place. Then she turned back to Luke, fixed him with a look of professional interest and got down to business.

"What's the last thing you watched on YouTube?"

The question was like being cross-checked from behind, leaving him momentarily stunned. No way in hell he was going to admit he spent his evening re-inflating his ego by watching her call him hot.

"Are you serious?" He'd meant to sound casually mocking, but was afraid it had come out somewhat closer to defensive. "That's the hard-hitting lead issue? You've got to have something better than that. What's the next question?"

She looked flustered by his outburst, and he hated the fact that he felt badly about it. He should be out on the ice, working on his slap shot, not in here trying to hide his guilt. She glanced down at her note card and closed her eyes, just for a second, before opening them and meeting his gaze. She looked focused, determined and a little defiant, if he wasn't mistaken. She cleared her throat.

"Boxers or briefs?"

All his composure deserted him. He held up a hand and glanced over at the camera. "Turn that off."

He waited until Jay lowered the boom mic and stepped toward the tripod before he rounded on the woman who had the singular ability to distract and frustrate him beyond measure.

"Look, I get that you have a job to do, but what's going on here, it's a big deal. This team is in the play-offs for the first time in its five-year history. Not a single player on our roster has ever won a championship. We've got a chance to do something great."

He took a deep breath and unclenched his fist.

"The problem is, two nights ago we handed Colorado a shutout victory on a silver platter. This team is now skating on thin ice, and if we're going to get out of the first round intact, I need my guys focused on winning hockey games, not talking about their underwear and eyeing your cleavage. Everyone else thinks you're cute and harmless and charming, but I don't buy it. So if you're just using us to make a name for yourself, then you've picked the wrong team. We don't have time for distractions right now. I'm done here."

With that, Luke stalked away from her. Again.

3

"LUKE! HOW DID it go? I was just going to stop in and get a behind-the-scenes peek at the interviews."

Luke pulled up short at the familiar booming voice. You didn't stalk past Ron Lougheed, general manager of the Portland Storm, no matter how frustrated you might be. Besides, this was the perfect opportunity to bring up his concerns.

"Yeah, about that, sir… As team captain, it's my job to make sure that my guys are centered, that hockey is the top priority. We've been through a lot this season and now it seems we're finally gelling at the right time. I'm worried that Holly Evans is a distraction we can't afford right now."

"Nonsense! Holly Evans and her delightful brand of infotainment is exactly what the franchise needs in order to make some headway into the hearts and minds of hockey fans."

Ron Lougheed was a heavyset giant of a man and despite his gregarious demeanor, everyone in the hockey world knew that when he made up his mind, there was no changing it.

Still, Luke had to try. "But sir, our time is better spent if we—"

"Let me tell you a little something about the business of hockey, Mr. Maguire. For the last five years, our merchandising and ticket sales have consistently ranked in the bottom third of the league's teams. Since we made the play-offs, we've seen a fifteen percent jump in merchandise revenue and we've almost sold out tonight's game. That's after *one* post-season game. We need to ride this wave, and the Women's Hockey Network is helping us do that. That clip of you walking away from her the other night has half a million likes. I'm not exactly sure what that means, but it's good."

Luke nodded. Shut his mouth. Braced for impact.

"I trust I don't need to tell you how *eager* we are to see results in the postseason?"

"No, sir."

"Excellent. Now, what were you saying about concerns?"

A headshake was the best Luke could muster. "Nothing, sir. Nothing at all."

"That's what I thought. I'm looking forward to watching your interview footage from this morning. After all, a captain sets the tone for his team, and I know I picked the right man to keep these boys on track. And put a couple of pucks in the net, while you're at it. Understood?"

"Perfectly."

Ten minutes of fuming and a chicken and pasta lunch later, Luke was back in front of the doors emblazoned with the stylized cresting wave of the team's logo. The doors burst open just as he reached for them, but instead of revealing his sexy, skirt-suited nemesis, he came face-to-face with the rookie.

"Dude, you up next?"

"Yeah." He glanced over the kid's shoulder, but the doors swooped shut before he could catch even a glimpse of teal. "Yeah, I'm up next."

"Cool. Word of advice? If you stand close enough during the part where she's on-screen with you, you can see all the way down her shirt."

When his tip failed to elicit any reaction from Luke, Sillinger's cocky grin faded. "Look, Cap, I want to apologize for what I said after the game the other day. Cubs explained why you're so tense and everything."

The kid glanced away as he said it, so he missed Luke's look of surprise at the mention of Eric Jacobs, or Cubs, as everyone on the team referred to him. "Exactly what did he tell you?"

"Oh, you know. All the pressure you're under from the higher-ups. And dealing with the media. And about your shot being off and stuff."

Luke exhaled. He should have known Jacobs would have picked up on all of Luke's behind-the-scenes crap. The guy was eerily intuitive—it was what made him so great out there on the ice.

"Um, you ever consider that maybe your shot's off because, um…" The kid leaned conspiratorially close and murmured, "I'm just sayin', maybe it would help if you changed the oil."

Luke stared blankly at the right-winger. He didn't like where this conversation was going, mostly because he'd been thinking about it a lot since he'd watched that damn video last night. Holly Evans was beautiful, and she'd made him think about something other than hockey for the first time in a long while. And she could certainly get him riled up. Not to mention she didn't give a damn about hockey. All things he found way too appealing at this very moment.

"Sometimes things get rusty when the pipe's not clean, you understand? I mean, how long's it been, man? In my experience, a good lube job can really help work out the kinks. And lucky for you, right through that door is a smoking-hot woman who told the entire internet that she considers you a certified Grade-A cut of beef. Plus, when I made my move, she told me she's looking for a guy with more maturity. That's your in, dude! She totally wants someone *old*. You should hit that."

Luke was pretty sure he'd never felt more ancient than he did having this particular conversation and he was only twenty-six. "Thanks for the advice, rookie."

"Hey, no problem, Cap. I got your back." Brett glanced at the door to the interview room. "You need a wingman in there, or you good?"

"I think I got it," Luke assured him.

Their conversation was interrupted by the infamous "Charge" anthem, a staple of sporting events everywhere. The rookie yanked his phone out of his back pocket. He glanced at the screen and grinned like he was on the cover of *Hockey Digest*. "Yes! It's the car dealership. You are not even going to believe the sweet ride I just bought!"

He was bouncing up and down like a Chihuahua that was about to pee on the floor. "The guys won't be able to give me a hard time about my wheels anymore. I gotta take this, Cap. Good luck in there."

Luke waited until Brett disappeared around the cor-

ner before he stepped inside for his mandated face-off
with Holly Evans, intrepid reporter.

"ARE YOU KIDDING ME, Jay? You took Salt Lake City
over Vancouver in the first round? That's ridiculous.
No wonder you always lose your hockey pool. I mean
honestly. I expected better of you. Vancouver clearly
has the edge and—Luke!" Holly bolted off the interview stool.

She hadn't been expecting *him*.

Like the rest of the team, he was wearing the navy
T-shirt that mimicked his jersey, with the cresting wave
on the front and his last name and number on the back.
His T-shirt even had a white *C* on the front.

But unlike the rest of the team, the sight of Luke in
his T-shirt and jeans did funny things to her hormones.
Seriously, is it hot in here?

"I thought you were…not coming back…ever. How
long have you been there?"

"Not long," he said, shoving his hands in his pockets
as he sauntered farther into the room. His cocked eyebrow and smug half grin said otherwise. Holly worried
that her attempt to appear innocent was failing miser-
ably, because her thoughts were anything but G-rated.

"What are you guys talking about?"

"You know," she said, so brightly that she could have
sworn he squinted a little. "This and that."

Luke nodded, glancing over at Jay, who avoided
meeting his gaze. "Sounded like hockey talk to me."

"What? No."

"Yes," he countered, matching her wide-eyed tone.
"It really did. I'm a bit of an expert on the subject. Salt
Lake City, Vancouver, first round. Definite hockey talk."

Luke had already nailed the fact that she was using this job to angle for a promotion. If she confirmed it by dropping the shtick, he could have her fired before she even got started. The best way to reassure him that she was harmless was to *be* harmless.

Holly's laugh was both forced and slightly manic as she shooed his words away with the dainty flick of her hand. "Oh, that. I was just telling Jay about…uh—" *Think, Holly. Think!* "—the numerology class I took." She nodded, warming to the story. "Yeah, really interesting stuff. I was explaining how it can help you make decisions about important things. Like which handbag to buy. Or in Jay's case, he's doing some hockey thing with his friends and I was showing him how he could use it to pick teams."

"Cool. I'd love to see how it works." He raised an eyebrow to punctuate the challenge, and she couldn't quite hold back her frown. But she'd come this far. Might as well go all-in.

Holly could almost swear she saw something like respect in his blue eyes as she lifted her chin and squared her shoulders.

"Uh, yeah. I just added up the letters in Vancouver— A is one, B is two and so on, your typical cipher—and then you take whatever the sum is, add those numbers together if it's more than a single digit and you have it. And in this case, *it* was equal to nine. Jay's birthday is September ninth, so obviously Vancouver is the luckier team for him."

Luke smiled, but it didn't quite reach his eyes. "So it has nothing to do with the fact that Vancouver is a team with enough depth and experience that it's pretty much a foregone conclusion that they'll knock Salt Lake out of the first round?"

Holly shrugged. "What can I say? The numbers don't lie."

"Sorry to interrupt…whatever *this* is, but I gotta use the can," Jay announced. "Down the hall and to the left?" he confirmed, and Luke nodded. The members of the Portland Storm were so superstitious that she and Jay had been asked to trek all the way to the building's public washrooms because no one but the team was allowed in the dressing-room bathroom on game day.

The two of them watched Jay leave, and she used the silence to regroup. She felt much more formidable when her adversary's baby blues swung back in her direction.

Until he said, "What is your game?"

"Game?"

His laugh was derisive, but kind of sexy for all that. "You're not fooling anyone. I know something's up with you and I intend to figure out what it is."

Oh great. That was all she needed, this handsome bastard messing up the most real-life, on-camera experience on her résumé. She might not like this job, but it was good experience, and she certainly wasn't going to lose it by making him suspicious on the second day.

"Up to something?" She placed a hand on her chest like a Southern belle. "Me?"

His parry was a narrowing of his pretty blue eyes. "Something has been bugging me about your act since the moment we met."

"Oh, you mean that time you were so unchivalrous as to walk away from me without answering my question?"

"So I asked myself," he continued, without missing

a beat, "why would someone who disliked sports so much that she asked about beards instead of the game bother to make a fake sports show? And the only answer I could come up with was, she wouldn't. The way I see it, you have your own agenda, and it's not going to do any of the members of this team any good."

Holly shook her head, eyes wide like an ingenue. "I don't know what you mean. The Women's Hockey Network is all about asking the kinds of questions we girls find important, such as what kind of cologne do you wear?"

He smelled so good she *was* actually a little curious.

"Oh, really? You're gonna keep up the act?"

Luke stepped closer. His big body sucked up all the oxygen, and her breath came faster to compensate. Who knew having a man accuse you of being smart was such a turn-on?

"That's the only question you want to ask me? I'll give you a free pass, on the record. Ask me anything. No holds barred. Nothing's off-limits. And I guarantee you a real answer. I promise not to say 'no comment.'"

Holly's hand clenched into a fist.

Any question. On the record. The reporting equivalent to winning the lottery.

She could ask about his brother's accident. Be the only reporter ever to get a statement on the one topic that was off-limits when interviewing Luke Maguire. Hear in his own words how it felt to be back in the play-offs for the first time since tragedy struck.

And she wanted to. She wanted to ask more than she wanted her next breath. But she wasn't supposed to know anything about hockey, so she restrained herself. Because if she took the bait, she would confirm that when given the opportunity, she'd put her ambition before the team. And she'd be done here. He could not only get her fired, but ruin her career. She had to keep her eye on the prize. She had to believe that one day, she would earn that story from him on her own merit, not as blackmail, and it would be worth the wait.

So she did what was best for her career and took a deep, centering breath. *Man, he really does smell amazing.* "Seriously, is that the new Hugo Boss fragrance?"

He narrowed his eyes and the crease between his brows deepened. It made him look even sexier, if that was possible.

"I've got my eye on you, Evans."

Not exactly the part of him she *wanted* on her just then, but probably the safest of the available options.

"I'm going to figure out what you're doing here and I'm going to expose you."

Geez. Everything sounded sexual when he was standing this close. She upped the ante and took a half step closer to him—she definitely wasn't going to let him intimidate her in this sexy game of cat and mouse they'd embarked on. If he thought she was going to let him be the cat, he was so very wrong. She'd been holding her own in a man's world for a long time.

"You can try, but there's nothing to expose. What you see is what you get."

"Oh, I very much doubt that, Ms. Evans. The truth is hiding somewhere behind that big hair and tiny suit."

"Look at me, Mr. Maguire. You honestly think there's room to hide anything under this suit?"

Her breath stuttered at the sudden fierceness in his eyes, the predatory gleam that pinned her in place. Were their lips getting closer because he was leaning in, or had she swayed toward him?

She was drawn to his body, hard as iron and just as magnetic. Her fingers brushed his biceps as his hands made first contact with her waist. She didn't want to stop looking at him, but her eyelids grew heavy as their breaths comingled and his lips moved closer, closer still...

"Okay, I'm back. What'd I miss?"

"Nothing!" Holly and Luke sprang apart at Jay's intrusion. Her heart thumped with a cocktail that was one part adrenaline and two parts unassuaged lust. She tugged at the bottom of her blazer, sneaking a quick glance in Luke's direction. He exhaled and rubbed a hand across the back of his neck.

Guilty. They looked as guilty as a couple of teenagers who'd been caught making out. Which they probably would have ended up doing if not for Jay's poor timing.

"Geez, Jay. You've been gone long enough. Let's get this interview going, shall we?" Her hand went to her hair—a classic Holly-ism that gave away her nerves. Good thing Luke didn't know that, she decided, dropping her hand. Luke lifted an eyebrow and Holly was sure she was blushing. Damn it.

"My pleasure," Luke said.

Jay, however, was not fooled in the least, and the look he shot her said she owed him an explanation. She waved him behind the camera and directed Luke back to the stool where their interview earlier had gone so wrong.

This one went a lot better. She had to hand it to him—he was as consummate a professional off the ice as he was on it. Charming, funny, quick with a witty answer. No one who saw this footage would dream for a minute that he believed her to be a threat to the team. In fact, the only question that tripped him up was "Do you have a secret talent?" She could have sworn he blushed a little before he stammered some nonsense about speaking a little French.

Then she sent him off to shoot some B-roll with Jay, which involved posing and puck tricks in the hallway.

For the first time all day, she was alone in the Storm's dressing room with a microphone in her hand. It was a pretty surreal experience, both as a hockey fan and as an aspiring sports reporter.

She'd watched it on television all her life, a reporter interviewing some member of the team or other, a bunch of bare-chested, sweaty-haired men talking about a big win or a battle-weary loss. The locker room looked different now, empty and quiet, all the jerseys clean and hanging number-side out, equipment neatly arranged on the shelves above each player's designated spot. Holly tried to just enjoy the moment, but her stupid heels were pinching her feet, reminding her that she was only living a fun-house version of her dream. But one day, she vowed. One day she'd be here, wearing pants and asking serious, in-depth questions.

And then Luke Maguire wouldn't be the only guy on the team who suspected that she was an expert on this stuff. Everyone on the roster would know she could hold her own.

She set the mic on the stool Luke had sat on for part of their interview and headed for the forbidden bathroom. Jay and Luke would be occupied with filming for at least five minutes. What harm would it do to sneak a peek?

It contained all the typical male bathroom accoutrements—urinals, stalls and a ginormous gang shower. But it was elevated to luxe standards by the details: gleaming navy and white tiles, stainless steel fixtures and enough accents of Portland Storm teal thrown in to pull it all together. Calculatedly masculine and very *go, team, go*!

Bracing a hand on either side of the sink, she stared into the mirror. She barely recognized herself. Gone were the usual blond ponytail and unadorned brown eyes. No T-shirt and jeans. She flexed her feet against the stiff leather of her heels—definitely no sneakers.

She wanted to splash some water on her face to assure herself the reflection in the mirror was just a mirage. But the sad reality was that the made-up, well-coiffed woman who was staring back at her now was the version of herself that had scored the biggest deal on her résumé by far.

This was the Holly Evans that was being invited to appear on local morning talk shows and well-respected podcasts. Hell, she'd even gotten a call about turning the Women's Hockey Network into a weekly comedy-sports show on satellite radio. And if fancy suits and a little lipstick were what it took to fulfill her dream of being a sports reporter, then it was a small price to pay. *Right?*

Holly sighed. This was who she was now, at least for the duration of the Storm's play-off run, and a splash of water wasn't going to change that. Besides, Paige had done such a lovely job with the goop on her face that she didn't dare. She settled for another sigh and tugged a few stray pieces of hair back into place before she headed for one of the navy stalls.

"Whatever it takes," she muttered to herself.

She'd just locked the stall door when the sound of footsteps made her freeze.

4

Aw, crap.

The footsteps were coming closer. Honestly. What were the odds? The bathroom had been deserted all day, and now someone decided to come in? Stupid hockey superstitions.

How could a bunch of grown men be this ridiculous? She was just wondering if perhaps there was a story in the naive belief wins and losses had anything to do with who used which freaking toilet, when her line of thought was interrupted by the "Charge" fanfare echoing off the tiled walls. The sudden burst of noise made her heart jump.

There was a muttered curse, followed by a hoarse, angry whisper: "Why are you calling me? It's game day. You know I'm not alone."

Her reporter instincts piqued, Holly abandoned all thoughts of superstitious nonsense and redirected her attention into eavesdropping.

"I'm very aware of that! But there's only so much I can do."

She frowned. She couldn't distinguish the voice, de-

spite all the interviews she'd conducted today. All she
could tell was that whoever had her trapped in a bathroom stall didn't have an accent. There were at least
fourteen guys on the team proper who fit the bill. And
that wasn't including coaching staff, cleaning staff,
anyone who—

"I know we have a deal!"

Whoa. Holly flinched at the anger in his voice. She
glanced down at her stilettos. Could she climb up on
the toilet quietly enough to not blow her cover? Because from that height, she could peek over the top of
the stall and see who the guy on the phone was. Not
an ideal solution, but at least it would give her a lead.

Excitement brewed in the pit of her stomach. Now
this was a story. Sure, she'd resigned herself to her fate
of asking moronic questions and wearing short skirts,
but maybe this was going to turn out to be a right place,
right time kind of serendipity. She lifted her knee to
test how high she'd need to hike up said skirt to make
the big step.

"No. No! You can trust me. I've got it under control.
You'll get your money's worth. We'll win tonight. Yes.
By two. I got it."

There was another loud curse and the sound of
shoes slapping tile as the man stormed out. Holly did
an about-face in the stall and unlatched the door, hoping to catch a glimpse of the man, but she saw nothing.
Damn it, I missed him.

But there, in the middle of the tile floor beside the
sinks, was a folded piece of yellow legal paper. Holly
rushed over and picked it up. It was a list of letters and
numbers in stark black ink. L2+, W2+, W1, W1, W2

and on it went. And suddenly the cryptic conversation made a lot more sense.

Well, well, well. It looked like someone was partaking in a little over/under betting. But who was stupid enough to do that?

Not only was it illegal for someone affiliated with a professional sports team to bet on themselves, but it would get you banned for life from the sport, and that was on top of whatever criminal prosecution was handed down. And to risk all that on point-shaving? It was dicey at best, because no one player had full control over a hockey game. And yet, if you were favored to win anyway, there were subtle things you could do to make the game a little closer than it needed to be. Someone could have gotten cocky.

The Storm had already weathered a scandal earlier in the season, when the not-so-secret affair between captain Chris Powell and GM Ron Lougheed's trophy wife had become front page fodder. Lougheed and his soon-to-be-ex were currently fighting a pretty nasty custody battle in the courts—and in the media. This was the last thing the organization needed on its résumé, tainting its inaugural play-off run. But for Holly, it was perfect.

This was the windfall she'd been waiting for. Because breaking a story like this was the key to making herself the front-runner, not just for Corey Baniuk's position, but an on-air sports position at almost any station in the country. It was a first-class ticket to reporter legitimacy. All she had to do was figure out who the guilty party was.

She liberated her phone from her bra—she'd had to stow it there earlier because skirt suits like this one didn't come with pockets—and snapped a photo of the questionable list so she could inspect it more closely when she got home.

The key to a good investigation, her mother had told her once, was to let the action go on around you. If you disturbed things too early, you'd never get the answers you were looking for. To that end, she refolded the paper and placed it back where she'd found it.

It was the first time during this entire sham that Holly felt she might have made her mother proud.

Her head whipped around at the sound of a door swinging closed. Getting caught now would ruin everything.

She hurried back into the bathroom stall as quietly as her heels would allow. Was it her perp returning to the scene of the crime? Had he realized he'd dropped his list? Maybe this time she could catch a glimpse of whoever was striding into the bathroom.

She'd just pulled the stall door shut and was about to navigate her way up onto the toilet—no easy feat since there was only a toilet seat and no lid—when an indecipherable noise made her stop. There was a beat of dead silence, and then, "Holly, I know you're in there. I can see your shoes."

Busted.

She unlatched the door and did her best to appear sheepish. "Luke. Hey. I didn't hear you come in. You look nice. When did you get a chance to change? I thought you were filming puck tricks with Jay."

The surge of adrenaline at getting caught morphed into a surge of something else as she took in the sight of Luke Maguire looking big and handsome and powerful in the most beautifully tailored charcoal suit she'd ever seen. His silk tie was a deep plum and his blue eyes were flashing. "We finished up a while ago. I've already changed and done a pregame interview. Things move fast on game day. That's why I thought you were *gone*." He put particular stress on the last word.

Geez. How long had she been staring in that mirror? No wonder Paige was always late.

"Now maybe you can explain what the hell you're doing in here?"

She shot him a look that was all smart-ass. "It's a bathroom, Luke. Do I have to spell it out for you?"

He frowned at the joke, and she resisted the sudden urge to smooth his brow. Why was he so serious all the time?

"You need to get out of here, right now. Only the team can use the bathroom on game day." If she wasn't mistaken, he looked a little embarrassed when he explained. "It's a good luck thing."

"It's a stupid thing," she countered. "I'll never understand why elite athletes aren't more enlightened than medieval man."

"Well, you don't have to understand it. You just have to respect it. And keep your voice down! Guys are in and out of the dressing room this close to game time." He ran a hand through his close-cropped hair. "Jesus. Not even the cleaners are allowed in today. We've got to get you out of here before someone sees you. Come on." He reached out to cup her elbow, an old-fashioned gesture that took her by surprise. Holly was dismayed at the way her skin thrilled at the warmth of his fingers, even through the sleeve of her blazer.

She shrugged her arm from his grasp, an act of self-preservation.

Luke sighed, obviously interpreting it as an act of defiance.

"Holly, you remember all that stupid stuff you asked me earlier? I gave you the benefit of the doubt and I answered all your dumb questions because you were just doing your job. Now I'm trying to do mine, and part of me doing my job is making sure my guys are ready to play. Focused. And if maintaining a stupid superstition is what it takes to ensure we bring our A game tonight, then that's what I have to do. So do me a solid, okay? Even though it's silly, and inconvenient and probably makes no difference at all, *please* let's get out of here before anyone sees you?"

Holly had to look up at him, despite her four-inch heels and his lack of skates. When had he gotten so close? God, he was handsome, all tall and stubbly, his ocean-blue eyes pleading.

"Fine. Let's—"

"Shit. Someone's coming!"

Holly wasn't sure exactly how it had happened, but suddenly she was chest to chest with Luke inside the tiny bathroom stall, made positively miniscule by his large frame. She heard the telltale footsteps a moment later.

Luke scooped her into his arms, one hand around her back, his other forearm under her knees. He'd literally swept her off her feet, and the suddenness of it stole her breath. Her arms flew around his neck in self-preservation, and she was vividly aware of every inch of her body, especially the parts of her that were plastered against his broad chest.

She could feel his muscles beneath his suit jacket, enough to tell that they were barely straining under her weight. She shot him her best "what the hell?" glare through the onslaught of yum, and he gestured with his chin in the direction of her feet.

"Your shoes. That's how I knew you were in here."

He breathed the words quietly, his mouth so close that she could feel the exhalation against the sensitive skin beneath her ear. It tickled, and she turned her head to protect her neck. Suddenly there was nothing but a fraction of an inch's worth of air separating their lips.

His muscles flexed then, pulling her tighter to his chest and her breath came fast and shallow. Heat prickled over her skin and pooled in her belly. Her fingers clenched against the soft material of his jacket.

Holly had never experienced lust at first sight before, but man, Luke Maguire made her lust. She ran her hand up his chest, and he shifted his stance, but before their lips met, he banged his elbow against the stall. The thump reverberated through the bathroom, snapping them back into the present, and they froze, eyes wide.

They both cocked their heads toward the sink side of the stall, listening intently for any sign that they'd blown their cover.

After another moment of silence, Luke set her carefully on her feet. The lust hangover made Holly a little wobbly on her heels. He stepped forward and lifted onto his toes so he could see over the edge of the stall. "He's gone," he said, the words tinged with relief. They hadn't even heard him retreat.

Holly unlatched the door, and with a covert glance to assure herself they were, in fact, alone, took some tentative steps toward the sink. She paused for a moment, but the piece of paper wasn't on the floor, nor had it been kicked under the sink.

"No time for sightseeing, Evans." Luke's hand at the small of her back was warm and insistent. "Let's get out of here before you get caught."

They snuck back out to the dressing room, Holly letting Luke precede her so he could make sure the coast was clear. She wasn't four steps out of the bathroom before several members of the team strutted into the dressing room, bedecked in expensive suits and pregame gravitas. Luke sent her a "See? You really lucked out," kind of look.

Ass.

Then the "Charge" anthem sounded to her right. Holly's spine snapped straight as she watched Luke fish his iPhone out of the breast pocket of his suit jacket.

He glanced at the caller ID and that serious expression of his descended over his handsome face like a shutter. Holly decided she might prefer his pompous expression after all.

"I gotta take this," he said. She watched with interest as he turned away from her, shielding the call with his broad shoulders. "Why are you calling again? Seriously? Hold on." Was it her imagination, or did Luke glance in her direction. "Let me get somewhere I can talk."

The "Charge" fanfare? Why are you calling *again*? Pieces were falling into place and she didn't particularly like the picture they were forming.

Had it been Luke in the bathroom earlier? She'd just assumed that whoever had inadvertently held the two of them hostage had come back for his list. But now that she thought about it, Luke had definitely had enough time to pick up the wayward paper before he'd gone all foot fetishist on her and blown her hiding place.

That could be the reason he'd even noticed her shoes under the stall in the first place—he was bending over to pick up the list.

Holly strained to hear more of his conversation, but he pointedly disappeared back into the bathroom. To her dismay, there were too many team members in the swanky locker room now for her to follow. Still, the reporter buzz—that's what her mother used to call it—was zinging around her gut. She was on to something. Obviously Luke's regular deep baritone had sounded nothing like the whispered panic she'd heard earlier, but that ringtone was an indisputable clue, and one that she had to follow up on.

LUKE WALKED OVER to stand by the sinks, hating that his gaze went immediately to the stall he and Holly had hidden out in only moments ago.

But he couldn't afford to be distracted by sex right now. Harding Lowe was the kind of law firm that charged in the triple digits for phone calls like these, and with money as tight as it was, Luke had to pay close attention and cut to the chase. "What's so important?"

"I was going to wait until tomorrow to tell you this, but I'm worried it might hit the papers and I didn't want you to find out like that," Craig Harding informed him.

Luke's blood turned to ice. It was never good when someone started a phone call that way, but when it was your lawyer? Infinitely worse.

"What?" The word was flat, more demand than question.

"Brad Timmons is filing for bankruptcy."

Luke's face went numb. The asshole who'd put Ethan in a wheelchair, put his parents in debt, strained his family to the emotional breaking point time after time over the last three years, was going to screw them over again.

"Fuck."

The word echoed hollowly in the vast expanse of shiny white tile and empty navy stalls.

Luke wanted to punch something, but it wasn't worth the fine the Storm would levy against him if he did.

Jesus Christ, how had things come to this? He made almost two million dollars a year with his new contract and still it was all he could do to keep himself and the people he loved financially afloat.

Loans, renovations, lawyers, specialists, physio—it had all added up after the accident. His paycheck was all but spent before it got deposited. He was grateful he had the means to keep his family living a comfortably middle-class life despite their exorbitant bills, but the idea that the coward who'd put his little brother in a wheelchair wasn't going to have to contribute a dime to Ethan's recovery made Luke nauseous.

Timmons had already lucked out with his criminal charges. He'd been convicted of assault with a weapon for the crosscheck, but ended up with an eighteen-month conditional discharge, which meant he hadn't served any jail time and he wouldn't have a criminal record once his probation was complete. Now he'd found a way to punk out on financial restitution, too.

"Thanks for the heads-up, Craig. I'll take care of telling my family."

"Understood. I'll be in touch."

Luke hung up the phone. He would deal with the personal stuff later. Right now, he had to focus on his team. They were only two hours away from puck drop.

He reached into the inside breast pocket of his suit, exchanging his phone for a folded-up piece of yellow legal paper. He'd found it on the floor of the bathroom and recognized instantly what it was. That 5–0 loss had been brutal. The fact that it was predetermined made it cut even deeper. Luke shook his head against the proof clutched in his hand.

He couldn't believe any of his guys would do this. They'd battled too hard to get to where they were.

And yet…the entire premise of point-shaving and over/under betting was predicated on having an inside man, someone out there on the ice who could impact the game.

This was the last thing they needed right now. He'd only just put this team back together after losing their last captain in a blaze of scandal and lies. It had taken months of work to get all twenty-three players over the shake-up and focused on making the play-offs.

And look at them now.

The only bright spot in this rotten situation was that he'd been the one to find the betting sheet. At least this way he could deal with it internally—protect his team.

He didn't even want to think about how this would have played out if Holly had found it instead. She could've ruined their chance at winning the championship before it even began.

And he wanted that championship, not just for himself but for the team.

Each and every one of those guys deserved to hoist sports' greatest trophy above their heads, and he'd do whatever it took to make sure that happened.

For them. For himself. For his brother.

5

"We'll win tonight. Yes. By two."

The words still echoed in Holly's brain, hours after the final buzzer had sounded.

The Storm had handled their opponents with relative ease tonight, up 3–0 after two periods. Then at the start of the third, Sillinger had taken a bone-headed roughing penalty, Luke had fumbled the puck and failed to clear the zone, and seconds later, LaCroix had lost his chance for a shutout.

For a while, things settled down a bit, until Colorado scored to make it 3–2 with seven minutes left in the game. Things were looking grim for the list's prediction, and then Jacobs came out of nowhere, stripping one of his opponent's defensemen of the puck. He deked out the goaltender and put a wrister top-shelf to make the final score 4–2.

And the Storm won by two with eight seconds left in the game.

"You'll get your money's worth."

The eavesdropped whisper haunted her.

It could just be coincidence, she reminded herself. It

wasn't like 4–2 was an outlandish hockey score. And this was the first prediction on the list that had come true. She had nothing but suspicion at this point. Still, the words were on her mind as she conducted post-game interviews with the guys.

"Hi, everyone. This is Holly Evans of the Women's Hockey Network, reporting live from the Storm's dressing room after a big 4–2 win over Colorado tonight. I'm with Portland defenseman Doug Kowalchuk." She turned and held her mic in his direction.

"Doug, what do you think of the new jersey colors?"

On the ice, the burly D-man was a force to be reckoned with, but off ice, he reminded her of a big cartoon bear—imposing but nonthreatening. His grin was goofy and genuine. "They're great. Red and black is a really classic combination, you know?"

Holly couldn't quite mask the withering look on her face at his answer. She hoped Jay had zoomed in on the navy and teal jersey behind Doug instead of her face. *Seriously, this was her life now?*

"No, Doug. Not New Jersey's colors—I meant the Storm's redesigned jerseys."

"Oh right. Yeah. They're awesome. Go Storm!"

Holly forced a smile as she turned back to the camera. She could see Jay's shoulders shaking with laughter. "You heard it here, folks. Go Storm!"

When she was sure the camera was off, she let out a frustrated sigh.

"You're doing great," Jay assured her. "Who's next?"

Holly glanced around the scrum in the dressing room. She'd been hoping to sneak in an interview with anyone who'd made a direct contribution—be it positive or negative—to the final score tonight. She wanted to get an idea of their demeanors, a sense of their moods. But unfortunately, all four players that had risen to the top of her list—Eric, J.C., Luke and the rookie—were all big draws for reporters and had press queued up and waiting for them.

"I think we've got enough. Kowalchuk's was interview number five, and I'll do some highlight voice-overs later to cut with it. They only wanted a three-minute piece about the game, right?"

Jay nodded as he removed the camera from the tripod. "Yeah, that should be plenty."

"Okay. I'll catch you in about half an hour."

"Sure thing, Holly."

Now that she was off duty, she angled her way through the bustling dressing room toward the crowd around Eric Jacobs. He was known to be a little shy and incredibly humble considering the breadth of his talent, but he was always exceedingly polite to reporters and smiled easily. Holly hadn't seen him smile once tonight.

She listened in as Corey Baniuk asked Eric about his spectacular goal, but the handsome centerman seemed disinterested in the recap, a little tired maybe.

And though he made the Storm's PR department proud by saying all the right things—"Colorado played a great game and were worthy opponents," "I saw an opportunity and fortunately I was able to capitalize on it," "I couldn't have done it without my teammates"—there was none of the quiet intensity that he usually brought to an interview and his gaze wandered, like he was preoccupied.

Then the "Charge" anthem played, and panic flashed across Eric's handsome face. He turned away from the cameras and microphones being shoved in his direction and dug his phone out of the pocket of his jacket.

What the...? Eric and Luke have the same ringtone?

Eric's expression darkened when he glanced at the caller ID, as if he was expecting bad news from whomever was on the line. "Excuse me, please, I have to take this," he said to the group of reporters.

After Eric left, the reporters dissipated quickly, rushing off to grab quotes from other players before their allotted time in the dressing room was up.

Holly pulled out her phone and typed her observations into the memo she'd titled *SUSPECTS*. This investigation was the key to parlaying this farcical job into something she could be proud of, and every clue counted. To prove it, she added a note about the dark circles under Eric's eyes and the fact that his last-minute goal corresponded to the +2 win predicted by the list. And the ringtone, obviously.

"Texting or 'Candy Crush'?"

Holly started, almost dropping her phone at the sound of a voice so close behind her. "Oh, geez. Luke, you scared me!"

He jutted his chin in the direction of her phone. "Your thumbs were really burning up the keyboard."

She tucked the phone back in her bra, trying not to notice that his eyes tracked her hand, making the move feel far more suggestive than she'd meant it. "Oh, you know. Reporter notes," she said vaguely, hoping she was pulling off nonchalance. "So what's the story with the matching ringtones? You and Eric have some kind of 'linemates for life' pact or something?"

"Team building. Everyone on the team is using it,

kind of a 'keep hockey your top priority during the play-offs' type of thing."

"Your idea." It wasn't really a question so much as a statement. That was exactly the type of hands-on captaincy she expected from the man standing beside her. And also a huge hit to finding her guilty party, since it put everyone on the team back on the suspect list.

"Yes."

"That's great! Do you mind if I talk about that in the piece we're putting together? People love fun little details like that."

"Sure. I know you're all about the fun little details," he said pointedly.

Man, he was tenacious. Even after the sexually charged moment in the bathroom stall earlier, he wasn't about to let her off the hook. Holly had to admit, she liked that about him. And she really liked that this battle of wills they had going on made her feel as if he was talking to the real Holly Evans, not the persona she'd agreed to play. It restored her faith in men to see that Luke Maguire wasn't about to be derailed by some off-the-charts sexual tension. For the first time all evening, her smile was completely genuine.

"Well, I should probably go help Jay pack up. Good game tonight."

"No, it wasn't."

His candor stopped her.

It really hadn't been, but while she admired his honesty, she wasn't going to get tricked into revealing her cover. He might be a worthy opponent—his entire life was predicated on it—but when she put her mind to something, she wasn't to be underestimated.

Except in this case, she reminded herself, since her

entire goal was to convince him to underestimate her. To that end, she scrunched her face in a way she hoped might convey bewilderment. "What? But you guys won. Aren't you happy?"

"It'll do," he said simply.

"Well, I thought you guys were awesome." She couldn't tell if he was buying her enthusiasm.

Meanwhile, his big sweaty body and mussed-up helmet hair were making her remember those stolen moments in the bathroom earlier.

Focus, Holly! She made a point to slow her steps to a reasonable pace as she walked away, even though her thoughts continued to race.

Luke cared about his team. That was obvious. The question was, did he care enough about them to cheat? For some reason, Holly hoped that her investigation turned up nothing incriminating. At least, not on Luke Maguire.

LUKE WATCHED HOLLY walk away.

Normally, he would have been glad for the team's win, but since it had come at the price of the list being correct, he wasn't able to let himself enjoy it.

And Holly had sidled right up to Eric, the one who'd fulfilled the list's prophecy.

Luke had planned on talking to the centerman, too. Eric had seemed really down lately—quiet as ever, but in a different way. Like something was wrong. Like his heart wasn't in the game.

What were the odds that Holly "I'm not that into hockey" Evans had randomly chosen Eric to target… Luke didn't like the way their instincts were lining up. And her whole demeanor had changed when she thought no one was watching—the set of her shoulders, the look in her eye. It was as though she'd flipped the switch from bubbly to…almost predatory.

He recognized that look. It was the one reporters always gave him before they sank their teeth into him. The way they'd looked after Ethan got hurt. The way they'd come at the team after Chris Powell had been traded. Luke had learned many times over that you couldn't trust anyone whose livelihood depended on uncovering secrets.

So he'd circled up behind Holly, trying to see what she'd been typing so furiously. But she'd bobbled her phone when he'd spoken, and he hadn't managed a good look at the screen.

And then she'd turned to him, a little bit breathless, slightly flushed, and his hormones had surged like they had back in that bathroom stall. His objectivity had been effectively drowned in a tidal wave of good old-fashioned lust.

"What's up, Mags?"

Luke looked over at goaltender Jean-Claude La-Croix. Despite a long history together in the minor leagues, it wasn't until Luke had been traded to the Portland Storm after Ethan's accident that the two of them had really cultivated a friendship.

"Hey, J.C. Nothing. Just trying to get the inside scoop on what stupid interview questions we'll be enduring tomorrow. Because distraction is just what a team in play-offs needs," he added. The bitterness that laced his voice was genuine.

"Ha. Yeah, she's pretty hot, huh? If you're gonna be distracted, she's the way to do it."

Luke's head whipped toward his friend. He didn't

like the way that comment bothered him. It felt almost like…jealousy? "Do you trust her?"

J.C. seemed genuinely surprised by the question. "What's to trust, man?"

"You don't think she's up to something? As if she's putting on an act so she can snoop around?"

"Luke, be serious. Her latest question was, 'name the last show you binge watched.' I really doubt there's much to worry about here," J.C. told him. "Management hired her to be comic relief. Ask us softball questions to make us look charming and funny so we can sell more jerseys. It's not as if she's a real reporter."

"I guess. But doesn't it seem odd to you that someone with no apparent hockey knowledge would even bother to apply for this position?"

His friend chuckled. "Dude, she's a YouTube phenomenon looking to cash in on her fifteen minutes. And management is taking advantage of it. Don't overthink it."

"You're probably right." Luke frowned. "I just can't shake this feeling that she's more of a reporter than anyone gives her credit for."

"We all have enough trouble without searching for more. So keep your focus on the game and forget about this inconsequential stuff. We tanked the first game. Tonight we were out for redemption. There's a lot of series left. Keep your eye on the prize."

Luke nodded. J.C. was right. But for some reason, he couldn't get Holly out of his mind.

He *wanted* to see her again. He wasn't quite sure when it had happened, but he realized in that moment that sparring with her had become the best part of his day.

6

"CAN I TALK to you for a sec?"

Holly looked up from her notes about her latest piece—she was headed to the parking lot so the Storm players could answer silly questions and show off their sweet rides—to find J.C., hands shoved in his pockets, looking sheepish.

"Is this car tour optional? Because I'd rather not do it."

"Oh. You mean, ever? Or did you just want me to reschedule?"

"I mean ever. I just…there's some family stuff going on right now. I know you usually don't get through the whole roster when you're doing interviews, so I was hoping you could skip me for the car tour today. I'm happy to do the other part—the teammate question stuff."

"Okay, that's fine. I can pick someone else."

The relief on his face was almost comical, except that it was a little too extreme for someone who'd just dodged the fluffiest interview of all time.

"LaCroix! Quit flirting and go do your tour so the rest of us can get on with ours."

The rest of her interviewees were milling about the dressing room, waiting to head outside with her.

"Bite me, Kowalchuk. I'm not doing the car stuff."

"Ha! Of course you're wussing out!" Sillinger laughed. "Have you seen the piece of crap he's driving lately? Some low-end, old-man SUV. It's almost as bad as Luke's truck!"

"You got rid of the Porsche?" Luke sounded genuinely surprised to hear. Weird, considering he and J.C. seemed quite close. Holly made a mental note to add J.C.'s vehicle downgrade to his suspect file.

"Back off, guys. You do your interviews and let me do mine."

There was a bite to the usually affable goaltender's voice, and judging by the looks on his teammates' faces, Holly knew she wasn't the only one who found it odd.

Sillinger wasn't cowed. "Hey, don't take it out on us just because you're cruising around town in an old guy's ride."

"Yeah, well, sometimes you gotta make sacrifices. Dads have to think about safety, not flash."

There was a long moment of silence as the not-quite-an-announcement sank in. Luke was the first to wade into the breach.

"Tania's pregnant? Congratulations, man! That's great!" Luke and J.C. shook before Luke pulled him in for a laudatory slap on the back.

"Yeah. Not quite the plan, but what are you gonna do?"

Holly watched as the Storm gathered around their goalie, congratulating him on the big news. A new baby on the way. That was a pretty good reason to sell your sports car, she supposed. Guess she didn't need to update the suspect file after all. Maybe she could score an exclusive on potential baby names, though…

"See?" crowed the rookie. "Dad vehicle. Just like I said. Come on, Holly. I'll show you what a real man drives."

"Says the guy who rolled up to his first practice in a Ford Fiesta," J.C. shot back.

"That was my old life. Now my ride lives up to my standards. Wait until you see it," he promised, bouncing like a toddler on a sugar high. "Cherry-red Lamborghini with black leather interior. It's so sweet, you might get diabetes just looking at it."

"Jesus, rookie," Luke warned. "You remember the first three years of your contract are flat-rate, right? Pace yourself or you're going to outspend your bank account before you start raking in the big bucks."

Holly hadn't even considered that. Sillinger was only making about three hundred thousand a year. Not chump change by any means, but it made it tight to rock two-hundred-thousand-dollar cars and a place to live, on top of day-to-day expenses. And the kid was not rolling in endorsement deals. Not yet, anyway.

"Don't you worry about me. If you got the fame, there's always a way to bring in the money."

Holly tried not to react outwardly to the sentiment, but she filed it away for parsing later. Under the guise of sending a text, she typed it into the Sillinger file on her phone, but when she glanced up, it was to find Luke watching her with narrowed eyes. She shot him a bright, innocent smile and followed the rookie out to his car. .

LUKE INHALED DEEPLY and let the cool scent of arena ice soothe him. The lights were off, except for a few spotlights shining down from the press catwalk high above and all the seats in the building were bathed in shadows. No one clapped, no one jeered, there was just the rhythmic sound of the cut of his blades echoing through the empty rink as he skated a slow, easy lap. To Luke, it was heaven, a balm to his battered nerves.

There was nothing better than a moment alone on the ice. It reminded him of his early childhood, before his family had moved to Oregon when he was nine. He'd spent many a Michigan winter outside, whiling away the hours pretending he was Gretzky or Hull or Lemieux on the patch of ice his dad had made for him in the backyard.

He'd needed this, a minute to himself, so he'd bailed on Holly's car tours, suited up and come out here under the guise of breaking in his new gloves. Truth was, he wanted to clear his head. Thanks to a neatly folded piece of yellow legal pad and a certain blonde in sky-high heels, everything was too complicated right now. One of his guys was putting himself ahead of the team by playing the inside man on a point-shaving operation.

And if Holly was aware of it and just waiting until she had enough evidence to expose one of his guys, he needed to beat her to it. It was imperative that he deal with this quickly and quietly. The Storm couldn't weather another scandal.

He snagged the puck he'd brought out with him as he skated past and bounced it off the boards to himself. He'd dreamed of winning hockey's ultimate prize for as long as he could remember. But now that he was finally back in the play-offs, his play was lackluster, at best. He needed to do better, play better.

He owed that to his team, who were counting on

their captain and looking to him to set an example. He owed it to his parents, who had sacrificed so much to support him on his hockey quest. And he owed it to Ethan. His little brother had always been the better hockey player, much as Luke had hated to admit it. But it had become obvious by the time the little punk turned ten that he was destined for big things. Even through his jealousy, Luke had always been proud of Ethan, cheering him on, pushing him harder.

And since Ethan couldn't be in the play-offs himself because of the accident, it was Luke's duty to succeed on his behalf.

Yet despite the pressure, and the hoopla, and his messed-up shot, Luke was having a hard time focusing on anything but Holly.

She was ballsy. He liked that about her. Most reporter types, though dogged, kept a reverential tone when they talked to the players, as if they were trying to butter them up. Not Holly. She was a straight shooter, which he appreciated. But it was also the reason he couldn't quite buy her ditzy routine. He'd met plenty of women who couldn't care less about hockey during his lifetime, and she wasn't quite pulling it off.

He'd been unwillingly impressed that she hadn't taken the Ethan bait, though. Despite all the red flags, he *liked* her. What was that about? He hadn't been "in like" with a woman since, well, since ever. "In like" was for mooning high school students.

All his recent relationships had been about good fun, good conversation and good sex…not necessarily in that order. But when it was time for him to suit up, hockey reigned supreme. So why was she always creeping into his thoughts now?

Luke stopped at center ice and sent the puck sliding toward the net, watching until it crossed the goal line and came to a stop at the back of the net.

Maybe Sillinger was right. Maybe it was just lust and he should get it out of his system. Maybe if he spent some time with her, he could break this ridiculous and ill-timed crush on the infuriating woman who kept popping into his mind at the most inopportune of moments.

He turned to leave the ice but stopped short. As if he'd conjured her, Holly Evans was standing in the players' box, arms crossed over her chest, waiting for him. And every single reason that he should stay away from her left his brain.

"You can't hide from me forever."

Luke skated over. "Who says I'm hiding?"

"You're the one out on the ice, avoiding the interview we're supposed to do. I'm the one who's here, questions at the ready, reporting for duty."

"You calling me a coward?"

"Hey, if the skate fits…"

He smiled at that, and her heart stuttered. She'd never seen him smile for real before. He'd flashed his PR smile on a couple of occasions during their on-camera stuff, but his real grin was something to behold. It was the first time he'd looked carefree. Like he didn't have the weight of the world on his shoulders. And it suited him. She had the irrational urge to make that smile come out more often.

"You think I'm gonna fall for some thinly veiled reverse psychology? I play hockey for a living. Trash talk doesn't faze me. You'll have to do better than that."

Luke stepped off the ice and over the boards like

they were nothing—God, why was that so hot?—and sat down on the bench. Holly turned her back to the ice and leaned against the boards, facing him. He set his stick against the side of the box and divested himself of his hockey gloves and his helmet. Then he ran a hand back and forth over his helmet hair. Somehow, after just a few careless swipes, his short brown coif looked photo ready. Holly lamented the hour and a half it had taken to make herself camera presentable.

"You don't like me very much, huh?" she asked.

"I don't like that you take the team's focus off the game and disrupt our routine. We need to be at our best, mentally and physically. I have to trust that every man on that ice is playing for me, and they have to believe I'm playing for them, too."

"Admirable sentiment, Captain Maguire, but there's really only one person you have complete control over. Sometimes you just have to keep it simple and play the game for you."

"I know exactly who I'm playing for," he countered. Then he went on the offensive. "So, Ms. Reporter, what kind of hard-hitting questions do you have for me tonight?" he asked, pulling his elbow pads off and setting them beside him. "What I ate for breakfast? The last song I downloaded?"

Luke pulled off his shoulder pads and jersey together and set the amorphous mound on the bench. Just like that, he was stripped down to a T-shirt—a T-shirt that was damp and clinging to his muscles. Suddenly his leg seemed very close to her bare thigh, and the fact he was wearing shin pads and hockey socks didn't deter a warm tingling from spreading through her body.

"Favorite sexual position?" he continued.

Oh geez. That warm tingling upgraded to hot throbbing in a split second.

He stood up. His skates made him incredibly tall. He loomed over her, but she didn't feel threatened. On the contrary, she felt sort of powerful—like she wanted to tame the beast. The smoldering look in his eyes said he'd let her. Somewhere, in the deep recesses of her brain, a warning light flashed.

She was here to do a job. She shouldn't get romantically involved with a story. Especially not a top suspect in a betting scandal that had the potential to rock the sports world. Her head knew walking away was the smart play right now, but her body overruled the call, especially since he'd provided the perfect opening. "So what *is* your favorite sexual position?"

His eyes darkened like a stormy sky. "Off the record?"

"Of course." Her words were a breathless rush.

"I like all of them." He reached for her, his big hands biting into her hips. She wrapped her arms around his neck as he hoisted her onto the edge of the boards and stepped between her legs. Her short skirt slid farther up her thighs, but she barely noticed the cold plastic against her skin. His mouth came down on hers, stealing her breath and wringing a moan from her.

God, she wanted him. Something about Luke Maguire called to every cell in her body.

Screw journalistic integrity, she decided. Finding out hockey players' favorite colors barely counted as journalism anyway. Then she stopped thinking altogether.

There was nothing but his lips against hers, his hands tugging her blouse from the waistband of her skirt and the sexy thrill of knowing that he was the only thing keeping her from falling onto the ice. Despite that imminent danger, she trusted he'd keep her safe.

He groaned as he slid his warm palm under her shirt and up the bare skin of her back. She returned the sound. The dichotomy of the cool, icy air and the warmth of his skin was a delicious push deeper into the sensual spell he'd cast.

She resented the T-shirt he was wearing and she tugged it up, revealing those washboard abs Paige had been so enamored with in the pages of *Sports Illustrated*. They were even better in real life, and Holly took pleasure in revealing each ridge, the definition of his pecs, his beautiful big shoulders and the flex of his muscles as he raised his arms so she could divest him of the shirt entirely. And then he was all naked torso and harsh wanting.

Holly couldn't get enough.

LUKE WAS OVERWHELMED by the desire inside him, clawing to get out. He was used to being in charge, but something about Holly unleashed the beast in him, made him want to lose control.

He let go, let himself drown in the lust, because he needed the escape. He needed her.

He wished he hadn't suited up, because there was no way he could shuck his skates, shin pads and hockey pants, but he wanted inside her too much to resist the desire. He ran his hand up under her skirt, groaning when he found her most intimate place.

He brushed his knuckles against the damp swath of her panties. She gasped and buried her face against his neck, her arms tightening around him.

Luke was certain he'd never felt more turned on in

his entire life while wearing so many clothes. There was something so amazingly sexy about the feel of her warm, smooth skin and the sounds of pleasure that escaped her throat, juxtaposed with the cool air and the familiar scent of ice and concrete that he loved so much. The heady scent of passion mixed with the comforting smell of the rink.

"Just so we're clear, this doesn't change anything," he panted. He pulled her underwear down her thighs. The first touch of his fingers on her clit made her stiffen. "I still hate that you interview my team like we're appearing in a teen magazine."

Slowly, he eased a finger inside her, and his gentle invasion was almost his undoing as he imagined himself sliding into her the same way. Her body, which had been tense, relaxed as he built her pleasure up. After a few strokes, he used two fingers to give her the friction she was craving so badly. His hips mimicked the thrust of his hand, increasing the pressure on her clit.

"Fair enough. And just so we're crystal clear," she breathed, arching toward him, unable to hold back any longer, "I'm still going to do it."

He could tell when he found her G-spot because she bit her lip and her fingernails dug into his back, pulling him closer. The sound of her breath grew choppy and it was the sexiest thing he'd ever heard. Until she moaned his name.

It short-circuited his brain and he sped the pace of his fingers, rubbing his thumb against her clit, moving his hand to the rhythm of her desire until she came apart in his arms, her cry of release echoing through the arena.

She sagged forward, her forehead resting on his

shoulder. He took a deep breath to calm his racing heart, but all he got was a lungful of her, a scent that was warm and female and sweet…like apples.

"That was amazing." Her smile was radiant, free.

He fought back a flood of testosterone that hit him so hard it was tough to think straight. He hadn't seen a smile like that maybe ever, and definitely not after sex.

The women he'd been with usually tried to act coy, or feigned modesty, or seemed embarrassed. Holly looked like a satisfied lioness who'd gotten exactly what she wanted.

"Paige was right. I definitely needed that."

He needed deep breaths and to not think about all the things they hadn't done together yet. "Who's Paige?"

"My best friend. She's been threatening to hire me a male escort because she's worried that my 'special flower' is crying out for some water. Her words, not mine."

Okay. Well, that *was as good a mood killer as any.* "She sounds like something else."

"Oh, she's something else all right."

A sudden crack followed by a loud hum echoed through the arena, and one by one, the big overhead lights fired up.

Luke swore as he, half-naked, and Holly, barely dressed, both instinctively dropped down behind the boards. It took him a moment to process what had happened.

"It's just the cleaning crew," he explained. He was about to get up, but when he looked over, instead of the panicked or angry woman he expected to find, Holly had both hands clamped over her mouth. "Holly?"

He was about to ask if she was okay when a giggle

slipped out from behind her fingers. Her shoulders were rocking and she was laughing so hard that Luke couldn't help but join her. God, she was pretty.

He leaned in conspiratorially. "Why are we still hiding?"

"Because my contract specifically states I'm not supposed to fraternize with members of the Portland Storm franchise. A clause, may I point out, that does not appear in my cameraman's contract."

Her put-out frown made him chuckle. "Well, they may not be a very enlightened bunch, but in management's defense, I've never seen Buchanan's practical white cotton panties." He grabbed said underwear from the ground beside his hip and held them out to her.

"Hey, these are really comfortable," she said, snatching them from his fingers. With a pretty blush, she glanced over at Luke's naked torso. "And touché. But I'd rather not get fired for engaging in an illicit affair with a member of the team because we were stupid enough to let the cleaning staff catch us."

"Is that what this is?" Luke asked, grabbing his T-shirt from the bench and pulling it back on. "An illicit affair?"

"This," she said, "was a mistake. A big one."

She had a point. He'd let her goad him into losing control. And boy, had he lost it. Yet he couldn't quite bring himself to regret it. Or stop himself from imagining Holly in his bed.

"I still owe you an interview. I'm going to head back to the dressing room and grab my stuff. Give me a couple minutes' head start so that no one suspects anything, and I'll meet you at the exit to the player parking lot."

"Aye, aye, captain."

She made a face at him before she hurried out of the

box and down the hallway with speed and stealth, despite her high heels.

As she disappeared around the corner, Luke leaned back against the boards, relishing the bracing sensation of cold plastic against his overheated skin. He'd never admit it aloud, but that had been the most genuine fun he'd had in a hockey arena in ages.

HOLLY WALKED THROUGH the parking lot beside the man who was responsible for her first non-self-induced orgasm in over a year. And thanks to his prowess, she found him even more attractive, something she wouldn't have thought possible before he'd unleashed a tsunami of delicious endorphins in her system. She'd forgotten how freaking fantastic sex could be. Holly vowed in that moment she'd never let herself forget again.

She couldn't help stealing glances at his handsome profile as they headed toward his black Ford F-250 pickup truck. Holly knew it was his because it was the last vehicle left in the fenced-in players' parking lot. He walked her over to her side of the vehicle and pulled the door open for her, and she crawled up into the black leather cab, waiting as he headed around to the driver's seat.

Get it together, girl. Time to focus.

"So," he said, crawling into the bucket seat beside her, "this is my truck."

He looked nervous, like he cared what she thought. She smiled and let him off the hook. "It's nice."

His answering grin was tinged with equal measures of relief, pride and embarrassment. The combination was utterly adorable.

"It's my one real indulgence. Money's been tight, so I try to keep the extravagances to a minimum."

Holly frowned. She was trying to keep it light and in standard Women's Hockey Network territory, and he just kept dumping incredible openings in her lap. Luke's latest contract was for just south of six million dollars over three years. How tight could money be? "Not a sports car kind of guy?"

Luke shrugged. "Can't haul a wheelchair in a two-seater."

Luke and Holly both froze at his slip. The blatant reference to Ethan hung there for a long moment. And after what they'd just shared, Holly felt she couldn't ignore it. "I read about what happened to your brother. I'm incredibly sorry for what your family has been through. What you've been through."

A weird pressure filled the cab. It was like she could feel Luke withdrawing into himself, but also fighting not to. She wasn't at all sure which part of him was going to win until he rolled his shoulders and tipped his head from side to side, like a boxer loosening up for a match.

After a deep breath, he finally spoke. "Yeah, it's been a tough couple of years. But Ethan's a fighter. And you don't want to hear the sob story. So how exactly does this work? You're just going to ask me some questions?"

Oh right. The interview.

"Yeah, if you can turn on your interior light, I'll just ask you about the truck, your first car, your favorite song to cruise to, that kind of stuff." She gave him the rundown while she pulled her phone out. Once she switched it to video mode, they were ready to roll. He was a good sport, and they sped through the questions.

Holly was just leaning toward him to show him the playback when the "Charge" anthem struck again.

"Sorry." Luke pulled out his phone. She couldn't quite read the expression on his face when he read the screen. "I have to take this."

She nodded, surprised to find he didn't leave the truck to answer the call. "Hey, Dad. How are you? Oh. Yeah, I heard. I was going to call and fill you in, but... uh..." He snuck a glance in her direction and flushed. "Practice ran late."

The G-rated reference to her amazing orgasm made her flush a little herself.

"Yeah, yeah. Don't worry about the money. It's covered. No problem. How's Ethan doing? Really? Well that's good, right?" He listened for a bit longer and then said his goodbyes.

He sighed and turned to her. "Sorry. That was my dad."

"Yeah, I got that." She smiled.

"Are you parked around here?" he asked, searching the near deserted parking lot.

"No, I caught a ride with Jay because my car's in the shop. It's okay, though. I'll just grab a cab."

"I'll drive you."

He looked as surprised as she was by the offer. "Oh. Well, if you're sure it's no trouble."

Holly told him her address and the big engine rumbled to life as he turned the key. She fastened her seat belt as the black behemoth rolled out of the parking stall under Luke's guidance.

"Sounds like you and your dad are close."

He shot her a look of surprise as he pulled out of the lot and onto the road. Night had fallen, and the roads around the arena had cleared.

Luke nodded. "Yeah, he's great." There was a smile in his voice that let her know he meant what he said.

The distance ticked by in ribbons of light and dark as they sped past streetlight after streetlight. There was something soothing about the calm quiet of the evening. It seemed to invite conversation, and Holly found herself saying more than she meant to, as though the residual physical intimacy they'd shared earlier was still lurking, searching for another outlet. "I'm jealous. My pop and I don't really get along that well."

"Nothing in common?" he asked.

Not for lack of trying, she thought, not proud of the bitterness that seeped in as she remembered the hours of her childhood she'd spent camped out on the couch, watching sports with her father, learning player names and stats, anything that might engage him in a more meaningful dialogue than, "What should we order for supper tonight, kids?"

"Well, he really loves his hockey."

"Is that why you took this job?" he asked, and she wondered at that.

Indirectly, she supposed, it was the reason behind every job she'd ever held. It was definitely the reason she strove to succeed in sports reporting. She craved her father's acceptance so blatantly that she was sure any psychologist worth her salt could pick her out of a lineup. Add that to her mother's long shadow, and it was pretty clear what drove Holly.

"Yes. Mostly. I stop by his place once a week to make

him dinner. I'd hoped maybe it would give us something to talk about."

It didn't work any better now than it had then, though, which was why she always timed dinner duty to coincide with a game she was covering for one of her freelance writing gigs—hockey, basketball, baseball— didn't really matter.

Keeping track of the game and taking notes for her articles always made the uncomfortable silence pass more quickly.

"I thought this job would impress him," she confessed. "But it hasn't. I'm not sure what the problem is. Maybe he hates the questions as much as you do. Before my mom died, I remember doing a lot of stuff with him. I miss that."

Holly often found herself wondering if her earliest memories were actually memories, or just dreams she made up of what a great family they'd been before cancer had stolen so much from her. "I want to ask him why we don't hang out or talk the way we used to, but I always chicken out."

Luke nodded as they took the exit that led to her neighborhood. "That's not just you. For the most part, my dad and I get along great, but family emotions can be tough to navigate. There's stuff I can't bring up with him, either." He paused. "Sometimes I worry that my parents blame me for what happened to Ethan."

Oh, God. Holly hadn't seen that coming, and it hit her like a kick to the gut. Did Luke really harbor that much guilt over an event that had been completely out of his control?

"The whistle blew. The game stopped. There was no warning when the hit came," he whispered.

He did a double take when she put a comforting hand on his arm. The startled look on his face, like she'd pulled him out of a memory, made her wonder if he'd meant to say that aloud.

He cleared his throat, motioning toward the upcoming turnoff. "This is the one?" he asked, effectively shifting the rest of their drive to a strictly navigator/navigatee dynamic.

When they rolled up to the curb in front of her house, she did her best to remove any pity from her smile, despite her breaking heart. "Thanks for the ride."

"No problem." To her surprise, he switched off the truck. "I'll walk you to the door."

They sauntered in silence up to the porch, side by side, in the chill of the night air. Their footsteps and the faint sound of distant cars were the only break in the quiet until they arrived at the front step. Her keys jangled as she pulled them from her purse and unlocked the door.

"Thanks so much for the ride, Luke. I really appreciate it."

"Not a problem. I just wanted to make sure you got home safe."

"And here I am," she said, motioning at her surroundings. "Safe."

"I guess I'll see you when we get back from Colorado then."

She nodded, and there was a weird moment where she wasn't sure if he was going for a hug or a handshake, and somehow it morphed into a bit of both, with a surprise cheek kiss thrown in for good measure.

"Good night, Holly."

"Good night."

With a smile, Holly stepped inside and pushed the door closed behind her. She dropped her purse and keys on the small table in the entranceway. Tonight had been…incredible. From the sexy encounter in the players' box, to laughing with Luke without a care in the world, to navigating some emotionally dense daddy issues while he drove her home.

Even the awkward cheek kiss had been kind of perfect. In a way, it was representative of this crazy friend-or-foe relationship they had going on. And suddenly, and with complete clarity, she knew that if she didn't do something, right then and there, to foster whatever fragile, new thing had bloomed between them tonight, then it would be lost forever.

She yanked the door back open with two hands, ready to run down the street after his truck if she had to.

Instead, she found him standing on the step, arm arrested in knocking-position.

HE'D BEEN ABOUT to rap on the door when she'd suddenly pulled it out of the way.

Luke had meant to leave, he really had, but he'd barely made it down the steps before he'd turned around. The prospect of being alone tonight was too much. Not with all that family stuff bubbling up in his brain.

He'd told her things he'd never said to anyone on the drive to her house. And the crazy part was, he was glad it'd been her.

She was addictive. A life raft in the midst of the sea of hockey that had overtaken his world. And tonight he wanted to be selfish. He wanted to do what he wanted, not what he should—consequences be damned.

"I can't stop thinking about you." He stepped toward her. And then his hand was buried in her hair, and his lips were devouring her lips, and she was pulling off his jacket as he pushed the door shut behind them. And for the first time since the Portland Storm had made the play-offs, Luke felt like he could breathe.

He was vaguely aware of the slap of his leather jacket hitting the floor, but suddenly her arms were around his neck and she was kissing him. His mind went incredibly, deliriously blank. With a growl of need, he grabbed the backs of her thighs and hoisted her into his arms, reveling in the press of their bodies as she wrapped her gorgeous legs around his hips.

"Which way's the bedroom?" he managed to ask when they finally came up for air.

"Over there," she said with a vague motioning of her head. He interpreted the gesture to mean he should turn down the hallway to their left. "Then last door on the right."

Their mouths met deeply, frantically, as he did his best to navigate without bumping into anything. He was eager to arrive at their destination but not willing to miss any part of the journey. There was something so elemental about carrying a woman to bed, kissing and touching and driving each other crazy. Luke couldn't get enough of it.

But inevitably, even through the halcyon buzz and the rushing hormones, Luke's responsible side made its presence known as they rounded the corner into her bedroom. "Please tell me you have condoms."

"Um…" She pushed her hair back from her face, brown eyes glazed with lust, lips swollen with his kisses and the rasp of his stubble.

He'd never wanted anyone so badly in his life.

"I don't think so. But I'm on the pill. So if you're…"

She trailed off, and he nodded reassuringly. "I am. In my line of work, we get tested for everything—and I mean *everything*—regularly."

"I am, too," she said. "Clean, I mean."

Luke stood there, with Holly wrapped around him, and there was a breath of anticipation in the air as they enjoyed that split second of awareness that what they both so desperately wanted was about to happen.

And then that moment of restraint erupted into all-consuming flames. He crushed her mouth with his own, lowering her onto the mattress and following her down. They tugged off each others' clothes, revealing the bend of an elbow, the curve of a hip, the camber of a thigh until finally they were both naked.

She was as beautiful as he'd imagined, as he'd remembered, as he'd hoped. The kind of beauty that brought a man to his knees.

He pushed inside her, one long, deep stroke, and then, because he couldn't wait, he did it again. And again. Losing himself in the rhythm, taking everything he'd craved since they'd gotten down and dirty on the rink boards, loving that the reality of their bodies together was putting his fantasy to shame.

He braced himself on his elbows, trying to tell if she was as turned on as he was, if she liked it, if she was pissed that he'd gone straight for the main event and cheated her out of foreplay. But when he slowed the pace of his hips, she opened her eyes and whispered, "Don't stop. Just like that, Luke. Just like that."

His cock surged inside her and he increased his pace,

loving the soft, startled gasps of her pleasure and the bite of her fingernails against his back.

He buried his face in her neck and breathed, "You feel so good, baby. You make me feel so good."

HOLLY WAS BEWITCHED. Luke Maguire at peak concentration was a powerful force. It was like every cell of his body was focused on her, a visceral awareness that crackled in the air. Missionary was not usually enough to build such a powerful arousal in her, but already she could feel the telltale heat growing, throbbing. She dug her heels into the bed and met him thrust for thrust, ensuring she was taking every inch of him inside her.

She'd thought his fingers had been magical, but this, the heat of him between her thighs, the weight of him against her breasts, this was so much better.

The orgasm at the arena had been sharp, tingly and shallow, racing along her skin like flash paper. In short, nothing compared to the savage need that was building inside her with every stroke of his cock, every brush of his hands. She wanted more, and when she couldn't bear the scorching heat of it a second longer, she let go, reveling in the dark pleasure that erupted, thick and hot like lava, through her veins. All she could do was hold on, clutching Luke against her as their bodies shuddered with the aftershocks of the explosion.

7

"I THINK I HAVE a crush on my arch-nemesis," Holly confessed to Paige a few days later.

Holly did not add the fact that her arch-nemesis was a virtuoso in the sack and might be involved in illegal betting. Just because some of the Storm's games had correlated with the list didn't mean they all would. And this was not an accusation that could be made lightly.

"First of all, thank God. It's been a shockingly long time since you've had man problems." Paige popped the last bit of her cupcake in her mouth and pushed the plate to the edge of their usual table at Piece of Cake, a cute little bakery just down the street from Paige's salon. Holly had originally dragged Paige to the shop in a moment of pure fangirlism, because it was owned by none other than Eric Jacobs's grandma, but the legendary vanilla bean cupcakes kept them coming back time and time again. "And second of all, who?"

"Just this guy at work. He's trying to catch me in the charade. Thinks I know more about hockey than I'm letting on and he wants to figure out my angle. It's awful."

"Then why are you smiling?" Paige asked.

"What? I'm not smiling." But she was. Holly did her best to neutralize her expression.

Sure, Luke was gorgeous, but she shouldn't feel so infatuated. She knew it was a trick—the result of her parent issues. After she'd lost her mom, her father had never thought she was good enough, no matter how much sports trivia she memorized, no matter how insightful her comments. He'd never taken her seriously. And as for her mom…it was really hard to impress someone who wasn't even on this corporeal plane.

So to have this hockey god, a player she deeply admired and respected on the ice, with a body and a face that made her melt, to have him see through the facade that she was presenting, well…of course she was infatuated.

Still, she couldn't get too carried away. He'd been sweet the next morning, even made her breakfast. On his way out, he'd kissed her and said he'd see her after the team's away games in Colorado. But he hadn't exactly professed his undying love, or even promised to call.

Besides, she was the one who'd insisted it was a mistake. And then there was that pesky contract thing…

"Okay, now you're seriously frowning. What's up?"

"I dunno, Paige. It was just really hot."

Paige gave her a skeptical look. "What kind of hot? Taming-the-rebel hot? Corrupting-the-innocent hot? Wrestler hot?"

"What? Ew. No. What is wrestler hot? That doesn't even exist."

"Wrestler hot is when the guy is loud and confident and is kind of pulling off fringe. Besides, you know I love it when men glisten."

Holly took a sip of her macchiato. "It was black-and-white movie hot. Sexy banter, witty repartee…"

"Everyone was wearing all their clothes…" Paige joked.

Rarely had Holly hated her fair skin and propensity for blushing more than she did in that moment.

"Oh my God! Someone watered your special flower? Holly, I'm so proud of you!"

She winced. "Geez, Paige. Decorum much? Would you keep your voice down?"

"Fine, but only if you tell me *everything*."

"He's the only person who doesn't treat me like a complete idiot. He basically accused me of stepping on the Storm to get ahead and that he's sure I know more about hockey that I'm letting on."

"Ooh. I like a man who gets to the point. So what did you do?"

Holly shoved a hand through her hair with a sigh. It felt so much better when it wasn't teased and sprayed into submission. "Swore up and down that I definitely *was* an idiot and then doubled up on the act. I can't let him win! Besides, why does he care so much whether I'm asking his team some joke questions? What's he hiding?"

Besides, of course, a potential windfall of ill-gotten cash for selling out his team.

"Oh, my! Sex *and* intrigue? This is more serious than I thought! Give me every detail about the man who swept you into bed."

Holly tamped down the blush as best she could. She was not getting into the down and dirty in the middle of a crowded bakery. "He's tall, and handsome and serious, but in this appealing, cares-about-something kind of way. And he's built. Good God, the body on that man." Holly took a long, restorative gulp of caffeine.

"So what's the problem? You deserve to blow off some steam. I know this job has been a little tough on you. So if he's into it, have at him!"

"It's not that simple. We both work for the team."

Paige sighed. "Stupid ethics. They get in the way of all the best stuff. Can't you guys have a secret affair or something?"

Holly laughed at the wording, so similar to her own. "That's what I love about you, Paige. You're always full of ideas."

She smiled back. "Please. You held my hand throughout my divorce. Getting you laid is the least I can do."

"You don't think it's wildly unprofessional of me?"

Paige shook her head so hard that her ponytail swung side to side. "No way! First of all, they called you because you're a YouTube sensation and they wanted to hitch a ride on your star. They know they're beyond lucky to have you. And secondly, this is a temporary job, not your career. So if there's a hot guy who will get you back in the game, then I see nothing wrong with that."

"Back in the game?" Holly laughed as Paige took a dainty sip of espresso. "What, you're sporty now?"

"*My* inspirational speech, *my* metaphor. All the men I work with are gay. I'm living vicariously through you here."

"Excuse me?" said a voice from above them.

Holly and Paige glanced up to find a woman standing beside their table, a young girl in tow. Holly pegged the girl at around nine. She looked very nervous, the pen and napkin clutched in her fingers shaking enough to betray the tremor in her hands. "Aren't you Holly Evans?"

"Yep, that's me. Can I help you?"

The woman's smile turned radiant.

"I'm Lydia, this is my daughter, Teagan. We just love your show! Teagan was actually hoping to get your autograph." Lydia gave her daughter a little shove, and the girl held the napkin and pen out in front of her.

"Of course!" Holly made herself speak through the shock. She accepted the napkin and smiled at Teagan. "So you like sports?" she asked, scrawling a quick little message and adding her signature to the bottom. The girl just shrugged shyly and took the napkin Holly held out to her.

"Can I get a picture of you two?" Lydia asked, holding up her phone.

"Oh, sure!" She leaned in closer to Teagan, surprised when the little girl tucked right in beside her.

"Oh, that's a nice one! Thank you so much. Teagan, say goodbye to Holly."

Teagan threw her little arms around Holly's neck, and Holly was so surprised, it took her a moment to hug the girl back.

"Thank you for making my mom yell less about my daddy watching sports," she whispered. "I want to be just like you when I grow up." Then Teagan pulled away and gave Holly a timid smile before she hurried to her mom's side again.

"How adorable was that?" Paige gushed. "What did she say to you?"

"She said she wants to be like me when I grow up."

Paige placed a well-manicured hand over her heart. "I think I just died a little from cuteness!"

The shrill ring of her phone shook Holly out of the surreal moment, and she grabbed it from the back pocket of her jeans. "Jay, what's up?"

Her tablemate made a face and Holly rolled her eyes at the childish gesture. *Grow up*, she mouthed, and then said into the phone, said, "I'm just having breakfast with Paige—hey. Be nice."

Paige frowned at the unheard insult.

"What? Are you serious? When? Oh my God. Thanks for the heads-up! Yes, of course I'm going to submit my résumé right now. Yeah. I'll talk to you later. Thanks again."

"What? What's going on?"

"Jim Purcell finally retired!" The announcement came out a little high-pitched and squealy, but Holly was so stoked she didn't even care.

"Oh my God!" Paige seal clapped with glee. "Who is that and why do we care?"

Holly laughed. She and Paige might be polar opposites, but she couldn't ask for a better, more supportive friend. "Jim Purcell is the sports anchor on *Portland News Now*."

"Right! The old guy with the bad toupee."

"Exactly. And if he's retiring, that means that the one and only Corey Baniuk is most likely getting promoted to the anchor desk as we speak. And that means…"

"That they will be looking for an amazing, knowledgeable, well-spoken replacement—who is you!" Paige's seal clap was genuine this time. "We have to get you home immediately," she exclaimed, downing the rest of her espresso. "You need to email that stellar résumé of yours to them at once. At once, I say! And then later, I'll take you out for dinner and we can celebrate this big step in your quest for nightly news dominance."

Holly smiled, appreciative of Paige's enthusiasm. "A lovely offer, but I'm having dinner with my dad tonight."

"Fine. I'll eat alone. But I'm having champagne in your honor and you can't stop me."

Paige's over-the-top zeal was a nice little ego boost, but Holly couldn't afford to lose sight of the truth. There were a lot of résumés out there far more stellar than hers.

But, she rationalized, if she could be the one to break a certain hockey scandal wide open at just the right moment... that was exactly the sort of thing that could make her stand out from a crowd.

"Hey, Pop. How's it going?"

"I'm still alive."

The gruff response was a typical one, and Holly sighed as she stopped at her father's recliner and pressed a kiss to his forehead. "Well, at least you've got that going for you. Tacos okay tonight?" she asked, heading toward the kitchen.

"I could eat a taco or two."

"Perfect. Put the game on and turn it up so I can hear it from in here." Holly hefted the bag of groceries onto the counter and set about unpacking. She put the hamburger in a skillet, sliced up some toppings and dumped the cheese in a bowl, glad she'd sprung for pre-shredded.

The third game of the series had ended with an uninspired 1–0 win for Portland. She knew that because she'd ghostwritten no less than seven articles about it. Not that she was complaining. Play-offs were always a nice bump to the bank account. Tonight they were playing the second of their two-game road trip. Which meant that, except for televised interviews, she hadn't seen a certain hot captain in a few days. She missed him.

But tonight she had to focus on the game and on Pop. Judging by the announcers' lack of enthusiasm, the Storm seemed to be headed for a scoreless first period. She hoped the second period would bring more excitement, because she had another seven articles due bright and early in the morning.

What could she say? Freelancing was not the most glamorous lifestyle. You wrote what people wanted, when they wanted it. That was why she preferred op-eds. It was nice to inject a little personality and analysis into a piece every now and again. But she couldn't afford to be too choosy. It was the no-frills assignments that paid the bills.

Whenever the cooking permitted, she snuck a glance at the big TV, her father's only real indulgence. Everything else in the small bungalow was almost exactly the same as it had been when she'd grown up here. Same oatmeal-colored carpeting, same dated brass lamps, same crystal knickknacks sitting in exactly the same spots, as evidenced by the dust.

It was a house full of good memories and dismal reality. Before her mother had died, the place had been cheery and full of love. Since her passing, it had gotten stuck in time, and there was a palpable desperation to a house that seemed to just be waiting for someone who was never coming back.

With a sigh, Holly served up two plates of soft tacos

and headed into the living room to join her father. She took her usual place on the threadbare couch after she handed him his supper, which he accepted with a grunt. "Pop, you think maybe it's time to get some new furniture?" she asked, noticing that he'd finally given in and duct-taped the armrest on his recliner. "You know, spruce the place up a little?"

"It doesn't need sprucing."

"Your chair is falling apart. It's older than I am."

"I fixed it, didn't I?"

Holly sighed. There was no budging him when he was being stubborn. "Like trying to charm a pig outta mud," her mother used to say, although to Holly's recollection, Diane Evans had always managed to get her husband to come around to her way of thinking.

Holly hadn't inherited that particular gift, so instead of arguing with her father, she dug in to her taco.

As they waited for the second period to get underway, the station was showing highlights from another game being played that night. A San Jose player tipped the puck into the opposition's net, and the home crowd went wild.

"Montana's gonna blow it. Those guys can't get their defense in order." Her dad's words were muffled by a mouthful of taco.

"I don't know. Federov and Rogers are a pretty good duo when their forwards are hot."

"Your brother thinks they should trade 'em both."

Holly shook her head. "No way. If they're going to trade anyone, it should be Powell. He's not living up to his potential because they don't have anyone good enough to play with him. But he's had a decent enough season, so they'll get something in return for him. Plus, he's got a real attitude. He's not gelling with the team."

No comment. Of course. Instead of acknowledging the brilliance of her strategy, he took another giant bite of his taco.

She watched and reported on sports for a living. Her brother was an electrician. Why *wouldn't* Neil's comments hold more weight?

Holly took a sip of her beer. It wasn't unexpected, but it always stung. She couldn't figure out why she kept setting herself up for the TKO, but at some point on these visits, she always brought up sports and always got shut down.

You'd think I'd have learned by now.

For a long time, Holly had figured her father's distance had something to do with her being a girl. Maybe he couldn't relate to her without her mother there as a buffer. And that sucked. But then her niece Melissa had come along and wound her grandpa around her little finger. He went to her hockey games and cheered louder than anyone. It hurt.

As they settled into watching the second period, Holly grabbed the notebook she'd set on the small table next to her dad's chair and began taking her usual game notes. It didn't take long before she found herself nitpicking the game, though. Well, not the game so much as the players. More specifically, the players she most suspected of game tampering.

Holly started an impromptu plus/minus tally on all the potential suspects from the last game. Brett Sillinger, for a boneheaded penalty, Luke for coughing up the puck, Eric Jacobs for a heroic play that had maintained the two-goal lead. It was more in-depth stat keeping than she usually bothered with, but then again, this was about more than a couple of "last night in hockey" reports. This was about making a name for herself in the world of sports.

Each time one of them was on the ice and the Storm scored, she gave them a plus sign. If one of them was on the ice and Colorado scored, she marked a minus sign. When the final buzzer scored to herald a 3–2 win for the Storm, Eric was +1 and Luke and the rookie were both sitting at -2. Not up to the season's standards for any of them. Which wasn't to say that bad games didn't happen. Still, trends were tracked for a reason.

"I thought these guys would walk all over Colorado. None of them are playing up to snuff."

Holly nodded at her father's summation. "You're right. Even when they win, they're performing statistically worse than I'd have suspected."

Her father harrumphed. "I'm going to get another beer. You want one?"

"I'm good, thanks."

And for once, Holly actually was.

She glanced at the stats filling the left side of her notebook—the list had been right about the spread again tonight.

She might not be great at family stuff, but she was a damn good reporter. And soon, she'd have the evidence to prove it. Even if that evidence pointed at Luke.

LUKE LOOSENED HIS tie and tried to rearrange himself in a more comfortable position in the posh airplane seat. Both games had turned out just like the list in his pocket had predicted.

He glanced around the dimly-lit cabin. In fact, the

mood was pretty low-key, despite their back-to-back wins in Colorado. Probably because they'd eked out some pretty ugly victories against a team they should have crushed. He was still surprised they'd held on to a 3–2 win tonight.

J.C. was snoring beside him. Most everyone else was plugged into a movie or talking with seatmates. Except for Eric, who was sitting toward the front of the plane, all by himself, reading a book, as usual.

He liked Eric Jacobs. He was a great hockey player, and the game really mattered to him.

And he was low-key off the ice—no tabloid stories of drunken debauchery or chronic womanizing. He didn't love being on camera, but he didn't complain about the obligatory interviews, either. Still, he'd seemed particularly aloof lately.

With the weight of his *C* heavy on his chest, Luke got up and walked over to him.

"Mind if I sit down?"

Jacobs glanced up from his book. "Sure." He opened his right hand to reveal a chain looped through two expensive-looking rings. Luke watched as he placed the necklace reverently between the pages of his spy thriller like a bookmark before shoving the book in the pocket in front of him. "What's up, Mags?"

"Actually, I was going to ask you the same thing," Luke confessed, taking a seat.

"Nothing really." Eric ran a hand through his dark blond hair. "I'm fine."

"Cubs, we both know that's bullshit. How long have we been playing together?"

"Two years."

"Exactly. You think I can't tell when something's up with my linemate?"

Eric was toying with the bottom of his matte gray tie and refused to meet Luke's stare.

"Let's not make this any worse than it has to be. Just be straight with me. You know I've got your back. Are you in some kind of trouble?"

There was a long, ominous stretch of silence. The piece of yellow legal paper weighed heavy on Luke's mind.

Then Eric heaved a sigh of defeat. "It's nothing like that. It's just…family stuff."

Luke kept his gaze steady and waited.

Cubs dropped the end of his tie and turned to face him. "My grandma's in the hospital. She had a heart attack."

"Jesus. Eric, I'm really sorry to hear that." Eric's parents had died when he was really young, and his grandmother, Stella Jacobs, had raised him ever since. She'd become the unofficial grandma of the Portland Storm and when she was in the stands to cheer them, a round of cupcakes from her bakery always made their way to the dressing room to announce her presence. "Is she going to be okay?"

Eric shrugged, and the gesture had an air of help-lessness about it. "The doctors won't say. She seems to be doing better. She pretty much forced me to come on this road trip." He smiled a little when he said it, and Luke had a vivid vision of tiny, white-haired Stella bossing her six-foot grandson around, even from the confines of a hospital bed.

"Why didn't you tell anyone?"

"I don't want to talk about it. And I definitely don't want reporters asking."

"I understand wanting to keep the family stuff under wraps. I won't object if you're sure you want to keep playing."

There was no hesitation in Eric's nod. "It's the play-offs. And I get that this is stupid, but I want to win for her, you know?"

Oh, Luke knew all right. It was what drove him every single day. He wanted that championship, wanted to win it so badly. Not for himself, but for the brother who'd lost his shot at the dream they'd shared their whole lives. "Yeah," he said quietly. "I get that."

And he did. Which was why he was so shocked when Holly's voice echoed in his mind. *Sometimes you just have to keep it simple and play the game for you.*

THE TEAM WAS already out on the ice for practice when she arrived at the arena the day after the Storm had knocked Colorado out of the play-offs with a 4–2 win at home. Because of the celebration and the increased media interest, the team captain had been too busy for her to snag an interview last night, but today, well, it was only a matter of time before they ran into each other, and her nerves were on edge for the reunion.

Holly was standing in the players' bench—Orgasm Central, as her dirty mind had taken to calling it. She was trying to keep her voice even, her blush under control and her eyes from wandering over to the practice happening on the ice behind her. Not because she cared about the practice but because of the overwhelming desire to check if maybe Luke was having as much trouble concentrating as she was.

It took three tries before she managed to get through the intro to the car interview montage without messing up. She could tell Jay was relieved when she finally nailed it by the speed at which he was gathering his video equipment. "Okay, I'm just going to run upstairs to get a few more angles on the practice. Give me ten minutes and we can go for lunch."

Holly nodded. "Okay. I'll text Paige and tell her we'll be at the restaurant in about half an hour."

"Aw, Paige is coming?" Jay whined.

"Suck it up, Buchanan. You know she is."

"Fine. Not sure why we have to ruin a perfectly good lunch, though. I'll meet you at the car in fifteen minutes."

She pulled her phone out of her bra, its usual storage space when she was dolled up in a skirt suit, and texted their ETA to Paige.

Her friend immediately returned the text with one that predictably read: Aw, Jay is coming?

"Holly."

She almost dropped her phone at the sound of the familiar deep voice saying her name. With a deep breath to restore her composure, she turned around. Luke, sweaty and gorgeous in his Storm practice jersey, was standing on the other side of the bench. Her stomach lurched at the sheer handsomeness of him. Clearly her body was ready to start on Orgasm Central: The Sequel.

"Hey. I didn't know we had interviews scheduled for today."

"Oh, we don't. Jay wanted to get some practice footage, and we filmed a quick intro to the car interview bit."

Luke's eyes darkened in a way that shot heat right

through her core. So apparently she wasn't the only one haunted by the sexy ghosts of lovemaking past.

He shook his head slightly, as if to clear it, and when his eyes met hers, he had the air of a man who'd come to a decision. His next words confirmed what that decision was.

"Look, I wanted to ask, do you think maybe I could buy you dinner tonight?"

Holly wouldn't have been more shocked if a hockey-stick-wielding alien had burst through the logo on his broad chest.

"As per my contract, we can't really be seen cavorting about town," she reminded him.

He nodded. "I remember. I was going to suggest takeout at my place. I'll pick you up around five thirty?"

Holly cocked an eyebrow at the time.

"Play-offs," he reminded her with a grin and a shrug. "I've got curfew, so we'll have to get an early start."

Holly couldn't help but laugh. "Didn't I go on this date in the seventh grade?"

"Yeah, well. You pick a career that twelve-year-old boys dream of, turns out that sometimes you get treated like a twelve-year-old boy."

"So there is justice in the world after all," she joked. "It's not all big paychecks, fast cars and constant adoration."

"It's definitely not all that," Luke agreed, and she caught a somber note in his deep voice. Before she had a chance to examine it, he barged through the moment. "So I'll see you tonight?"

"Sure."

His smile was endearingly self-conscious. Not the smile she'd expected from a professional athlete blessed with a big salary and the good looks to back up some swagger. "I gotta get to practice. Five thirty. Don't forget."

Holly watched him skate off to rejoin his team, her phone clutched to her heart and a single thought running through her head.

Oh, shit.

8

"He asked me out."

"Who?"

"Luke Maguire."

The answer brought two very different reactions from her lunch companions. Jay stopped in the middle of eating his nachos, his mouth agape. Paige continued the act of buttering her roll and barely glanced up as she repeated, "Who?"

Holly took a bracing chug of Heineken. "The shirtless hockey player from the *Sports Illustrated* magazine your eyes were glued to a couple of days ago."

"The superhot dreamy one with the bedroom eyes and the washboard abs?"

"He's not *that* hot," Jay countered gruffly.

"Please. That man is a god."

Jay took a huffy bite of nacho.

"Wait a minute! Is Abs Maguire your sex crush?"

Jay cringed. "Do I really need to be here for this?"

"Hush, Jay. This is important lady business. So what did you say?"

"I'm not an idiot, Paige."

"Great. So if you said yes, then I don't understand the problem."

That was the more complicated part. "The problem is that a high concentration of shame is eating through my stomach lining as we speak." Holly took the final swig of Dutch beer. "I'm contractually obligated to lie to him…about my hockey knowledge," she hedged. She hadn't told either of her best friends about her suspicions of illegal betting, and the realization that she was lying to everyone she cared about made her feel worse. "I have a guilt ulcer."

"What's to feel guilty about? You're a beautiful, single woman, and he's a rich, single man who looks like he knows how to wield his hockey stick. Let's not kid ourselves, Hol. You need to get laid. Jay and I, mortal enemies that we are, have actually discussed hiring a male escort just to put you out of your misery."

Jay winced. "No, we haven't."

Paige's raised eyebrow confirmed that they had.

"I swear, you guys. How is it even possible to be so close to your dream job and yet light-years away?"

She reached over and took an unladylike gulp of Paige's red wine, then did her best not to spew it across the table. "Oh, *gawd*! How do you drink this stuff?" she demanded, gratefully tearing the bottle of Pilsner Jay held in her direction from his hand and drowning out the obnoxious taste of merlot with luscious, cold beer.

Shrugging, Paige took a perfect, dainty sip of her wine. "Well, I'm proud of you for putting your lady bits first for once."

"Oh, man! I'm trying to eat here," Jay complained.

"And vaginas disgust you?" Paige asked. "You can't possibly ingest food around women who are discussing them, even though men talk about their penises constantly?"

"What? How did my junk get brought into this conversation? Nobody said anything about dicks."

Holly groaned. "Would you two just sleep together already and get rid of the sexual tension? It's *exhausting*."

"Ewww!" Their disgust was expressed loudly and simultaneously. "That would be like kissing my—" The words "sister" and "dog" overlapped.

Their affronted expressions were almost identical, not that Holly would offend either of them by saying so.

"Seriously, Jay? Your sister? She has a mustache."

"Kissing me is like kissing a dog?"

"Except for the fact that I could muster some enthusiasm for kissing an adorable dog, yes, I imagine so."

Jay cocked an eyebrow. "So you *have* imagined kissing me, then?"

"You. Wish." Paige held up a hand. "I'm going to pretend you're not here." To Holly, she said, "I'm still not seeing the problem."

"Paige, game analysis isn't just criticism. There are a lot of moving pieces to a game. Line matchups, hot streaks, underperforming players, team morale. And when you get millions of dollars to play a game, you have to understand that there will be some scrutiny. But I'm a professional, and that means I can't let my personal feelings interfere with my ability to do my job."

Something that she would do well to remember, Holly decided.

Paige nodded, but Holly didn't like the sly smile on her face. "Tell me more about these personal feelings you're having."

"And now *I'm* going to pretend *you're* not here."

"You'd better be thanking your lucky stars that I'm here. Otherwise you'd probably end up wearing some ripped jeans, a ratty T-shirt and a ball cap on your date tonight."

Holly looked down at her stupid skirt suit. "Well, I'm definitely not wearing this."

Paige smiled. "I'm sure we can find a happy medium. Hurry up and finish your nachos, Jay. We've got work to do."

THERE WERE BUTTERFLIES in her stomach as she crawled into Luke's truck. He'd rolled up to her curb at five thirty sharp, just as he said he would.

"Wow. You look great."

The compliment meant a lot, because it was the first time she'd hung out with Luke feeling even remotely like the real her. Paige had sanctioned Holly's pick of a pair of dark-wash skinny jeans and a white T-shirt. But in exchange, Holly had relented and worn the strappy nude heels and the jade statement necklace Paige had insisted upon.

"Thanks. It feels like I haven't worn pants in ages."

"Well, to celebrate the Portland Storm making it through the first round of play-offs and your long-awaited return to wearing pants, we can have any kind of takeout you want."

"Wow. Living the high life."

Luke nodded as he pulled away from the curb. "Tonight, the world is ours."

Two hours later, Luke, Holly, two mostly decimated pizzas and two bottles of beer were spread out across the living room floor of Luke's swanky—but not quite as swanky as she'd been expecting—apartment. They'd just finished watching a chase movie that was heavy on explosions and fast cars and light on plot. Holly was pretty sure she'd never been on a better date. Until he said—

"I have a confession to make."

Holly's stomach bottomed out and she choked on her beer.

Luke's brow creased with concern. "You okay?"

She nodded, coughing as she set her bottle back on the coffee table. "Yeah. Just went down the wrong way. Sorry. You were saying?"

The nervous look on his face made her gut twist into knots. Her palms prickled with moisture.

No. Please don't let it be Luke who's throwing games.

"I had a bit of an ulterior motive for inviting you for dinner."

The beat of silence scraped across her nerves. She hadn't realized how much she was hoping Luke was innocent of point-shaving. And now, here they were, after an amazing couple of hours together, and it was all about to fall apart.

"Tomorrow I'm heading home to Millerville for the sledge hockey finals," he said, reaching for his own beer. "These kids have worked so hard. And if they win this weekend, they're going to the state finals. I told them I might not be able to make it, but now that we've wrapped up the series and I have a week off, I asked for two days' leave," he explained.

He picked absently at the label on the bottle in his hands and took a deep breath. "And I was wondering if you'd come with me."

Holly couldn't quite process the words. There was a buzzing in her ears as she reexamined the last few minutes. "You plied me with pizza and beer because you want me to go to your hometown with you?"

Luke nodded before draining the last of his drink and leaning forward. "I was kind of hoping you'd do a little story on the team. You know, interview them, give them a taste of what it's like to deal with the media. They'd love that."

Holly couldn't hold back a smile at how animated Luke was at the mention of the kids who were part of his pet charity. She'd done a lot of research about it for her Hockey Hottie of the Month shtick.

Kids on Wheels was a top-notch organization that did an amazing job assisting kids with physical disabilities. She admired the genuine joy on Luke's face when he talked about it. It made her want to say yes, except...

"I don't have anywhere to stay. And Jay's filming a wedding this weekend."

"My parents have plenty of room. And we can just film the interviews on my phone. It doesn't have to be fancy. I just wanted to give the team some professional hockey league experience, you know?"

Holly shook her head to clear it. *Did he just say what I thought he just said?*

"You want me to stay at your parents'?"

"Yeah, well, my mother would kill me if I rented a hotel room, so consider Casa Maguire like a bed-and-breakfast, but with more parental interference."

"You had me at breakfast." The words were out of her mouth before she'd realized she said anything. Because she liked Luke. She wanted to go with him. And it scared her that, for the first time in her life, she was willing to put her job—even one as banal as asking hockey players what kind of underwear they wore—on the line for someone else.

Thankfully, Luke's dazzling smile was enough to shore up her resolve against the doubt that was trying to trickle in.

"That's great. I was really nervous about bringing this up, but the kids are going to be so excited to meet you."

"Me?"

"Yeah, they've all watched your show. They give me a hard time about my answers to your interview questions. The second your videos get posted to the Storm's site, the text messages start pouring in."

"Ah. So this isn't a nice perk, this is revenge," she joked, before downing the last sip of her own beer.

"You caught me. Gotta keep those little punks in line or they'll be out of control before you know it."

"Ooh. You're such an authority figure. That's actually kind of hot."

"What can I say? It's dangerous when things get out of control," he said, and the proof was in the way his eyes darkened.

"It can be," Holly agreed. She shivered as he moved closer. His leg came into light contact with hers. Her body flooded with warmth and sweetness, like she had syrup coursing through her veins. He increased the pressure of his knee against her thigh.

"You done with dinner?" he asked, and his voice was low and rough.

She licked her lips involuntarily. "I could be talked into starting the dessert course."

"I was hoping you'd say that."

THE JOURNEY TO his bedroom was a hazy, erotic blur of kissing and touching and haphazard stripping. Now he was standing shirtless beside the bed, marveling at how damn sexy Holly looked in her pale-pink lace lingerie. He watched with slack-jawed appreciation as she crawled onto the mattress, giving him a perfect view of her incredible ass.

God, he'd never seen her in anything but sensible white cotton, and the idea that she'd picked the sexy lace out just for him was blowing his mind and his restraint. And that was *before* she rose up onto her knees, her back still toward him and sent him a coy glance over her shoulder. She reached behind her back and unclasped her bra, tugging it off in the most delectable little peep show he'd ever seen.

Shucking his jeans and boxer briefs in one move, Luke joined her on the mattress, pulling her against his chest. He nuzzled at her neck, kissing the curve of her soft shoulder. She turned her head to grant him easier access, raising her arms to run her fingers through his hair. The movement made her breasts lift, and Luke couldn't resist the pretty sight. She sighed her pleasure as he ran his hands up the smooth skin of her torso and cupped her breasts.

He pressed his erection against the small of her spine and she pressed back, as if she was testing how ready to go he was. She wouldn't be disappointed.

"I want you," she said.

Luke wanted her, too. He loved her abandon, the way she went after what she wanted, be it the answer to her question, or his body.

Her breath came in soft little pants, and he reveled in how responsive she was to every brush of his fingers, every kiss of his lips. He ran his palm down the front of her stomach, his fingers flirting with the elastic of her panties. She leaned back against his chest, encouraging him to explore. He accepted her invitation, sliding his fingers down to find her wet and ready for him.

"Jesus, Holly. I want you, too. So damn bad."

Her throaty, sensual laugh made his hips jerk. "So do something about it," she challenged, reaching forward so that she was on her hands and knees in front of him. She wiggled her ass, looking back at him over her shoulder.

Luke let himself take what he wanted. With a growl, he yanked her underwear down her thighs and, anchoring his hands on her hips, plunged into her.

OH, GOD. She'd never felt anything like this.

Holly had to remind herself to breathe, the pleasure was so intense. What was it about this man that could take her so high, so fast? She'd released the beast, and there was something so empowering about making a man known for his steely control lose all sense of restraint. He was stroking her G-spot with every thrust of his hips, and the sensation that was building inside her was all-consuming.

She dropped down to her elbows, almost screaming with pleasure as the angle changed. Heat streaked through every nerve in her body, culminating in a tingling starburst of bliss that moved through her body like a wave. Luke was only a few strokes behind, and she could feel him pulsing inside her as he joined her in the most intense orgasm she'd ever experienced.

Sweaty and satisfied, she flopped onto her side. Luke lay down beside her, gathering her close so that her cheek rested against his shoulder. She reached out to trace her finger around his nipple, loving the way his pec jumped at her touch. "So much for your curfew."

"What are you talking about? I was in bed by nine."

She laughed. "You always play this fast and loose with the rules?"

"Rules were made to be broken."

She snuggled up closer to his big naked body. "After that deft display, I can't help but agree."

He ran his hand up and down her arm, and the soft, rhythmic stroking made here eyelids flutter closed.

"I'm glad you're coming with me tomorrow."

"Mmm. Me too."

"Are you falling asleep?"

She smiled as he shifted, pulling the blanket from the end of the bed up to cover them. "Maybe."

He pressed a sweet kiss to her forehead. "'Night, Holly."

She wasn't sure if she answered or not as she drifted into the best sleep she'd had in ages.

9

SINCE SHE'D STAYED the night, they'd ended up getting a much earlier start than they'd anticipated—despite the fact that their tandem shower had turned into an hour and a half of fun distraction that had necessitated another shower.

Luke grabbed the bag he'd packed, and they swung past her place so she could throw some weekend supplies into a small suitcase. One more quick stop at her brother's house—Holly needed to pick something up, and Luke was nice enough to indulge her in the last-minute errand—and they were on their way out of town.

In a scant hour and twenty minutes, they pulled up in front of a house that was small but cozy. The kind of house that any kid would be lucky to grow up in. It boasted big trees that were perfect for climbing, lots of driveway space, which, considering two hockey stars had grown up here, had probably hosted its fair share of ball hockey grudge matches and an attention to detail—potted flowers, freshly painted trim—that said the owners cared.

The idyllic scene made her a little wistful. She couldn't

remember even a handful of family memories that could match the cheerfulness of Luke's childhood. She bet he could think of hundreds without trying.

Luke slipped the keys from the ignition and unbuckled his seat belt, but he paused after that, staring at the house for such a long time that Holly didn't know what to make of it.

"Luke?"

She'd startled him, but he tried to cover it with a smile. "Sorry. Lost in thought." He scrubbed a hand across his stubbly face.

Despite the question she'd asked him the day they'd met, Holly was glad he wasn't growing a proper play-off beard. That whole "lumberjack chic" look that was sweeping the magazines didn't do much for her.

He sat there for another long moment, as if he was psyching himself up to go inside. When he finally turned to her, his smile was dimmer than she was used to and it didn't quite ring true. "Ready?"

Holly did her best to seem peppy and normal, ignoring the part of her that wanted to wrap her arms around him and soothe the pain she hadn't expected to find in his eyes. "Ready," she agreed.

She followed Luke into the small bungalow where he'd grown up. She'd never considered meeting the parents to be the big deal everyone else seemed to make it, but suddenly her stomach seemed to think it was on a roller coaster.

"Holly! It's so nice to meet you!"

She found herself caught up in a hug that blindsided her. It took her a moment to relax into the other woman's maternal embrace. She couldn't remember the last time a woman had hugged her—*really* hugged her—as opposed to the cursory, two-second greeting hugs that were all the rage these days. It was…a little unnerving, actually.

"Thank you, Mrs. Maguire. It's great to meet you, too."

The tiny dynamo of a woman flicked her fingers, shooing away the notion. She was casually dressed in jeans and a yellow T-shirt with flowers on it. Her short brown hair was streaked with gray and cut in a no-fuss style that suited her kind face.

"Please. I'm just me. You're the famous one! I watch all your shows on the internet. Luke gave me an iPad for Christmas. I even saw your interview on *Good Morning Portland*. And we don't stand on formality here. Call me Cathy. This is my husband, Ross."

Holly smiled as she shook the man's hand. He had only a hint of white at the temples of his dark hair. It made him look very distinguished. She could see Luke in him: the strong nose, the kind eyes, the rugged jaw.

Luke's smile, though—his real smile—that was all Cathy.

"Well, let's not just stand in the doorway! Luke, you take Holly's bag up to my knitting room." She turned to Holly. "It's actually a little suite over top of the garage, so you'll have lots of privacy and your very own bathroom. I already made up the bed for you."

Luke caught Holly's eye and grinned at the way Cathy had subtly stressed that the room was for her and her alone. "Sure thing, Mom." Grabbing both their bags, he leaned over and kissed Cathy's cheek, and Holly was enchanted at the joy sparkling in his mom's eyes.

As Luke headed back outside and toward the detached garage, Cathy tucked Holly's arm into hers and pulled her into the kitchen.

The highly varnished wooden table was littered with official-looking envelopes emblazoned with the logo of a prominent bank in the top left-hand corner. Some of them had ominous red stamps that said *Final Notice* on them.

"Oh my. Please excuse the mess!" Cathy rushed over to the table and began stacking the notices into a disordered pile, but not before Holly noticed that Luke's name appeared on some of them, along with his parents'. *Huh*.

"Ross and I were just paying some bills before you arrived." Cathy dumped said "bills" into the shoebox on the table and replaced the lid. Only then did her smile regain its genuine warmth of earlier.

"Now let's get some food into you. I just finished making coconut gumdrop cookies—they're Luke's favorite."

The afternoon sped by. The Maguires were warm, attentive hosts, and although Ethan did not make an appearance, Holly was drawn in by their obvious closeness. Luke seemed more relaxed here, and she liked knowing that this side of him existed—that he wasn't uptight and serious all the time.

And yet, she couldn't help but notice the blatant hockey void in the conversation. Hours of chatting had gone by with no mention of Luke's play-off run, or anything hockey related whatsoever. Considering Luke's entire world revolved around the sport right now, she found the omission very odd. She found herself growing indignant on his behalf that his parents didn't make more of a fuss about him.

"I'm going to go check on dinner," Cathy announced. "Luke, why don't you show Holly to her room, in case she wants to freshen up before we eat. I've practically held her hostage all day. I'm sure she'd appreciate a moment to herself."

Holly smiled at the false summation of their day, but the prospect of stealing a few moments alone with Luke was too great to pass up.

"Actually, Luke, I'd rather see your old room."

LUKE LED HER down the hallway to his childhood bedroom. There was still a wooden sign on the door with a hockey player and his name printed in primary colors. He'd picked it out himself in the second grade. A normal kid probably would have taken it down when he was thirteen or fourteen, but at fourteen, Luke had already been billeting with other families and playing in the minor leagues, trying to become the best.

Ethan had been coming up fast on his heels, a definite hockey superstar in the making, and it had pushed Luke to excel. He was proud of his little brother, but he was also competitive enough that he didn't want to be surpassed, either.

As always, his room was just how he'd left it. His parents had talked about turning it into a reading room, but they'd never gotten around to it. Maybe that was something he should do for them for Christmas…send his parents on a trip somewhere and get the room renovated. Just a little something to put a smile on their faces. God knew they deserved it.

"Wow, check it out. A glimpse into the life of a young Luke Maguire." She meandered around the room, staring at inscriptions on trophies and titles on book spines.

He spent the moments looking at her. He liked casual Holly, barefoot and clad in jeans and a black T-shirt, her blond ponytail swinging behind her as she snooped around his room.

He thought it'd been the short skirt and push-up bra and teased-out hair that had pulled him in, but if he was being honest with himself, he found her much prettier and more alluring today than ever before.

He was curious about the attraction they shared. It burned hot and bright and yet it wasn't all passion. They'd had a great trip down, conversing easily and laughing the entire hour and change that it had taken to get here. He enjoyed her company, both in and out of the bedroom.

"Yearbook!"

"What? No!" Luke did his best to mask the panic in his voice, knowing that would only encourage her. "You don't need to look at…too late."

She was already nose deep in the glossy pages, in search of childhood embarrassment.

"Is this you? Oh my God, you had a mullet!" She flipped the yearbook around to show him, pointing gleefully at his photo, as if he didn't remember what he'd looked like.

"I did not have a mullet."

Her pretty mouth hitched up on one side, and he was a goner. "Photographic evidence begs to differ."

"I had a flow. It's totally different. That is a well-respected and timeless hockey haircut. Jaromír Jágr had that exact hairdo."

She laughed as she shut the book and set it on the end table. "Check out this place. You ate, slept and breathed hockey, huh?" He followed her gaze around the room—

old hockey trophies and medals dominated the shelves above his desk, along with a couple of hockey biographies and an impressive collection of *Don Cherry's Rock'em Sock'em Hockey* videos.

"Wayne Gretzky, Mario Lemieux and Bobby Hull." She pointed at each of the faded, curling posters he'd tacked to the wall so very long ago. "Dreaming of the day when you'd have a poster of your own?"

"You know it." Luke tried to keep the frown out of his voice as he crossed his arms over his chest.

Wayne Gretzky, sure, his 99 was showing after all, and Mario Lemieux's name was printed on the poster. But Bobby Hull? Would someone who didn't have the first clue about hockey recognize him? He seemed a little too niche.

It was on the tip of his tongue to call her out on it, but he swallowed his retort. He wasn't going there. No, he was done being suspicious. He liked this girl. She was funny and beautiful and he enjoyed her company. He was done looking for flaws and investigating her every move.

Being home always reminded him that things could change for the worse in a split second. And it would be a disservice to forget to enjoy the things he had. Because he was all too aware that it could all disappear in an instant.

"Instead of posters, I had a signed picture of Barbara Walters on my wall," she said.

Luke smiled at the odd choice. "Really?"

Holly nodded. "It was my mom's. She was an anchor on the six o'clock news. Barbara was her hero, too. Every weeknight, my family would eat dinner in front of the TV and watch Mom tell us about the day's events. And at the end of the hour, she'd tuck her hair behind her right ear and that was our signal. Her little code that she loved us and she knew we were watching."

Her smile was sad, but beautiful, and Luke was glad she'd trusted him with it.

"When she died of breast cancer, my father let me hang the Barbara picture in my room. I'd look at it every night and promise my mom that one day I'd be a reporter on TV, just like her, and then I'd tuck my hair behind my right ear so that she knew I was thinking about her."

"And that's why you do what you do," he said, adding a few more pieces to the puzzle that was Holly.

"That's why."

"I'm sorry about your mom."

She shrugged as she sat on his childhood bed. "It was a long time ago. And it's nice to remember the good stuff."

"Kids! Dinner's ready! Wash your hands."

Luke and Holly shared a smile at his mother's summons, and he took comfort in the fact that, even in the midst of constant flux, some things never changed.

"Take a seat! Holly, you can sit beside Luke over here," his mom directed. She set a roast chicken on the table.

"Everything looks fantastic, Cathy. Thank you so much for having me."

His mother preened under Holly's praises. Luke hadn't seen his mom this animated in a long time. "Oh, it's our pleasure. It's just so nice to see Lucas happy."

Luke didn't have a chance to be embarrassed, because the hum of the back door made everyone freeze. His father walked in first, and behind him, Ethan navigated his wheelchair into the kitchen with such ease that it made Luke realize just how long he'd been using it.

Sometimes it felt like only yesterday they'd been camped out in the hospital, waiting for the swelling to go down, hoping against hope that Ethan would walk again. Other times it felt like aeons had passed since that fateful night.

"The prodigal son returns," Ethan muttered when he spotted Luke.

Luke forced a smile, trying not to be hurt by the lackluster greeting. "Hey, little brother. Looking fit." Ethan's arms bulged against the fabric of his Nike T-shirt. He must be up at least a couple of pounds of muscle since they'd seen each other last. "Katie must be putting you through your paces."

Ethan nodded at the mention of his physiotherapist. "Yeah. She's tough." He grabbed his plate and started dishing out some food.

"This is Luke's friend, Holly," his mother offered, wading into the tension.

"Hey," he said without glancing up.

"Ethan! Manners." There was a warning note in Cathy Maguire's voice that not even a sullen twenty-two-year-old could ignore. Hell, even Luke still flinched when she marched it out.

Ethan sighed and Luke watched him physically regroup. When he raised his eye, Luke recognized the battle-weary look of a man engaged in a tireless fight. "It's very nice to meet you, Holly."

Holly's smile was warm, despite the fact that the greeting had been decreed rather than given sincerely. "You, too, Ethan."

Taut silence settled over the room then, broken only

by the clank of utensils as everyone served themselves portions of chicken and stuffing and gravy and veggies.

"If you'll all excuse me, I'm going to eat in my room."

"Ethan, we have company." Ross Maguire's voice held a hint of desperation that made Luke wonder how many nights he and his mother ate at the dinner table alone.

"Oh, that's fine." If she was hurt by his brother's abruptness, Holly didn't show it. "I understand better than most what it's like to want to avoid small talk," she joked.

"Thanks." It was, by Luke's count, Ethan's most sincere moment of the night.

The world deflated when he left.

Luke could feel his mother's heart break just a fraction more, see the way his father's shoulders sagged under the weight of his youngest son's misery. He wanted to punch his brother in the face for doing this to them, and yet…

And yet, Luke's own shoulders and his own heart were just as affected at the sight of Ethan's struggle to make sense of the devastating blow he'd been dealt. His little brother was the strongest man he knew. Ethan's dedication to his recovery was beyond incredible, and even the doctors were amazed by his progress. Luke was jealous of how ripped he'd gotten and in awe that Ethan had taught himself to walk again.

But he could only stand for short periods, and his walk was a slow shuffle. Neither was good enough for his brother, who was aiming for nothing less than full recovery. But three years later, the odds of that were dwindling at an alarming rate. And his brother was angry.

Luke couldn't blame him for that, even when he wanted to.

Holly broke the ice. "I can't wait to dig into this chicken."

His mom smiled and encouraged everyone to eat. Holly was wonderful through the entire meal. She did her best to carry the dinner discussion and after the meal, helped his mom clean up the dishes so he and his father could figure out why the power opener on the back door wasn't functioning properly. Then they all sat outside on the deck with his mother's famous lemonade and talked until it was time for bed.

"Thanks," he said, as he and Holly sauntered toward the garage. The evening air was warm and damp and tinged with the scent of spring flowers.

"For what?" she asked, like she honestly didn't know.

"For handling today like a pro."

"Nothing to thank me for. Your family was incredibly kind."

He put a hand on her hip, tugged her forward a step and brushed a soft kiss to her lips. Her sigh was sweet and dreamy, and he leaned his forehead against hers. "Good night, Holly."

She smiled up at him. "Good night, Luke."

He kissed her once more before he pulled himself away, glancing behind him to watch her ascend the small staircase and disappear into the guest suite.

He waited until she'd pushed the door shut before he headed back to the house.

He had every intention of heading straight for his

own room, but instead, he found himself standing outside his brother's.

Luke rapped his knuckles against the door before he pushed it open.

Ethan didn't look up from his physio log book. "Hey."

"Hey." It was weird, seeing the wheelchair beside the bed. Unlike his own room, Ethan's reflected the passage of time. All his trophies and posters and hockey paraphernalia had been packed up and hidden away—probably in the attic, if he knew his mother. Cathy Maguire couldn't bear to throw away memories.

"I just dropped Holly off in the guest room. I'm glad Mom's still protecting our virginities," Luke joked.

A ghost of a smile played over Ethan's lips.

"Some things never change."

Luke didn't mean for his gaze to dart to the wheelchair beside the bed, but it did, and the moment of camaraderie disappeared with the blank expression that overtook his brother's face.

Luke wasn't about to let his brother shut him down that easily. Not again. "And some things change a lot."

"Yeah, well. Be thankful you're the one who got out of this mess unscathed."

Luke ran a frustrated hand over his hair. The ever-present guilt chewed at the lining of his stomach. He ignored his brother's dig and tried to take the high road. "Do you want to come to the sledge hockey game with Holly and me tomorrow? The kids would love to meet you. They keep giving me a hard time that you haven't come."

"I have physio."

"Ethan—"

"I have physio," he repeated in a tone that brooked no opposition.

"Okay, fine." Luke didn't know what to do to reach his brother anymore. Every time he came home, he felt like they grew further and further apart. "You wanna have some ice cream?" he asked. It was a last-ditch effort to connect, a ritual from back in the day. Whenever there was company staying at the house, they'd wait until midnight and sneak downstairs for makeshift ice cream sundaes, thinking they were pulling one over on their parents.

It wasn't until years later that they'd realized it couldn't be coincidence that whenever they had visitors, there was always ice cream in the freezer and an array of toppings in the cupboard. Luke didn't doubt for a second they were there now.

"I think I'm just going to go to sleep. Hit the light on your way out?"

Even though Luke had braced himself for the impact of rejection, his brother's dismissal stung more than he'd expected. "Yeah, sure. Good night, Ethan."

Luke flipped the switch and headed for his own room. He unceremoniously stripped down to his underwear and crawled into bed, but he didn't sleep. It wasn't just that he'd outgrown the bed, either. The whole house was uncomfortable. The whole family was stuck in the middle of a nightmare.

Luke was still wide-awake come midnight. He slipped out of bed and pulled the door shut behind him. Once in the kitchen, though, he decided ice cream didn't sound all that appealing.

A glance out the window showed a light burning

brightly in the suite above the garage. Suddenly, he was in the mood for a different kind of sweet.

Luke grabbed the extra key from the hook in the entryway and was careful to close the door silently behind him—a trick he'd mastered by the age of twelve. In no time, he'd crossed the small expanse of grass between the house and the garage and climbed the stairs to the door.

He knocked before he used the key. Holly looked up from her phone as he pushed the door shut behind him. She was sitting on top of the covers, her back against the headboard, feet flat on the mattress, wearing nothing but a T-shirt and another pair of those sensible white cotton panties. She was absolutely perfect.

"To what do I owe the honor?" she asked, her eyes tracking down his bare chest, boxer-briefs and thighs. If he hadn't already been up for the main event, that once-over would have done the trick.

"This is a booty call."

She licked her lips. "You don't say."

"But it's not just any booty call," he explained, crossing the carpeted floor until he stood beside the bed. "This is a booty call twelve years in the making."

She set her phone on the end table. "Oh? Sounds epic."

Luke nodded as he crawled across the bed. "Since I was fourteen years old, I've dreamed of sneaking a woman up to this bed. Tonight, the fantasy has finally presented itself. So whad'ya say, Holly Evans? Want to make a man out of me?"

"I don't know," she told him, and the uncertainty on her face made him pause. She'd seemed into it a second ago.

"I don't want to get in trouble." She cocked a wicked eyebrow. "We'll have to be really quiet."

Jesus. Lust ignited in his belly as if her words were gasoline. He understood she was just playing along, teasing him, but damn if the role play wasn't working for him in a big way.

She twirled a piece of hair around her finger. "And you have to promise not to gossip to all your friends about this at school tomorrow."

"I promise." She was so damn perfect in that instant that the words came out in a growl. He hooked his arm beneath her knees, tugging her toward him so that she was flat on her back. She let out a cute little shriek, surprised by the move, and he swooped in to kiss the giggles from her lips.

"Shhh. Wouldn't want someone to figure out that I sneaked in here."

Her eyes shone with humor as she wrapped her arms around his neck and pulled him down on top of her. "Oh right. Well, I guess I should warn you, I'm a bit of a moaner, so you'd better think up some way to keep me quiet."

Up for the challenge, Luke pressed his mouth to hers. God, he ached to be inside her. Everything around here felt so wrong, but when he was alone with her... he could turn off his brain. He could just shut it down, run on pure instinct and lose himself in her embrace. It was almost magical the way she made him forget all the pressures that dogged him when she wasn't around.

He poured everything into that kiss, his whole self, and when she pulled away from him, things were spinning so fast that it took him a moment to reorient himself.

"Luke?"

He caught his breath, braced himself on his elbows. Her smile was so pretty it made his chest ache.

"I think I'm ready to go all the way," she teased.

He grinned down at her, unable to resist dropping a kiss to the end of her nose. It was the perfect thing to say. She'd kept things light, pulling him back from the spiraling emotional abyss of moments before.

He got to his feet beside the bed and shoved his underwear down his thighs. "I'm the luckiest fake high school kid on the planet," he said, watching as she sat up and tugged her T-shirt off. He enjoyed the gentle sway of her breasts as she wiggled out of the white cotton panties. At this point, those damn panties had some kind of Pavlovian hold over his body. Just the thought of them made him hard.

"Oh, you're about to get lucky, all right."

She reached for him as he joined her on the twin bed. But he misjudged the distance, swearing when he banged his head on the headboard as he pushed her back against the pillows.

"Oh, are you okay?" she asked, giggling as she ran her hand over his hair to soothe the wound. "I'm sorry. It's not funny," she said, but she was still laughing a little, and he couldn't help but join her, even though his head stung almost as much as his pride.

"If I die, it will be from embarrassment and not head trauma," he assured her. She scooted over to the edge of the mattress so he could lie down.

"Awww. Poor thing. Don't worry. Nobody's first time goes smoothly," she reminded him, reverting to their role play. It brought a smile to his face. "Maybe you'd better let me kiss it better," she offered, leaning over and pressing her lips to his.

Her mouth tasted heavenly. She ran her tongue across his bottom lip, and he reached up to bury his hand in her hair, pulling her toward him so that he could return the kiss with more urgency. He was panting when she pulled away.

"Did that help?"

He nodded. "That definitely helped…a little."

"Only a little? Hmm. We might have to up our treatment level." She pushed herself up and straddled his hips.

He could do nothing but watch in awe as she lowered her body slowly toward his erection. He was so turned on by the time his body finally made contact with the apex of her thighs, he was crazy with wanting.

She continued moving down, trapping his cock against his stomach before rocking her hips forward and back, her wet heat sliding along his length, driving him to madness.

"How about now?" she asked. There was a breathy quality to her voice that confirmed she was just as aroused as he was.

"What head injury?" he managed to ask, his hips pumping involuntarily in an effort to maintain the sensation that had wrung a groan from deep in his chest. She was going to kill him with pleasure, Luke decided.

"Shhh. You're going to get us caught."

She pressed a finger to his lips and he sucked it into his mouth. She threw her head back at the sensation and sped up the pace of her hips. It was incredible, but he wanted more. He wanted all of her.

As if she was reading his mind, Holly reached down and placed her hand on his heart, bracing herself so she could reach between them and when she finally slipped him inside her, his world shrank to raw sensation and a string of swearwords on loop in his head, because he couldn't form anything more coherent through the bliss.

Then she started fingering herself as she rode him, and he'd never seen anything so perfect in his whole life. It was all he could do not to explode. But he needed to hold out until he was sure she was getting at least as much pleasure out of this as he was.

"Come for me, Holly."

"I'm so close…so close."

He grabbed her hips, pushing himself as high and deep as he could. He thrust once, twice, and then she fell forward, hands on either side of his head, kissing him as the contractions of her body ignited Luke's own fierce orgasm.

10

"Good morning, Holly. Did you sleep all right?"

Surely the heat prickling across her face wasn't as obvious as it felt? This was another parental milestone she'd never endured. She'd already moved out of the house by the time she'd lost her virginity.

"I did, thank you, Cathy." She accepted the mug of coffee the other woman held in her direction and took a grateful sip.

"I'm glad to hear it. Come, sit down. I'm making bacon and eggs. I hope that's okay."

"Sounds delicious."

"Oh, wonderful. There's fresh fruit on the table, please help yourself. I'll bring the rest out as soon as it's ready."

"Can I help at all?"

"Nonsense! You're our guest. Besides, that's what Luke is for, right, son?"

Holly turned to find Luke padding into the kitchen in a rumpled T-shirt, gray sweats and a seriously sexy case of bedhead and stubble. "I live to serve," he agreed.

Her pulse sped up as he stepped toward her and pressed a kiss to her cheek.

Holly ducked her head to hide her blush. Cathy's smile of approval was too much to deal with right now. She hurried into the dining room, joining Ross at the table.

"Morning, Holly. Sports section okay?"

"Perfect. Thank you." She set her coffee down and sat next to Ross, accepting the newspaper he handed to her. Combined with the incredible spread of strawberries, pineapple, kiwi and grapes piled high on the platter in the middle of the table, Holly was hard-pressed to remember a lovelier morning. It was idyllic, the kind of scene she'd imagined so many times since her mother had died.

Seemed that Luke was not the only one living out childhood fantasies this weekend. The problem was, her fantasy was a dangerous one. This family wasn't hers and never would be. Still, she couldn't help but let herself be swept up in the idle chatter and homey sounds that came with eating breakfast with people who loved each other.

"You should see that apple tree your mother and I planted beside the ramp in the backyard last year, Lucas. We'll deal with these plates and then I'll show you how much it's grown."

"No, you two go," Holly insisted. "Take Cathy with you. Spend some time with your son. I'll take care of the breakfast dishes. It's the least I can do."

"That's very sweet of you, Holly." Cathy stood, but started gathering up plates as she did. "You boys go on outside. I'm going to relish the joy of having another woman in the house. And don't you argue with me, missy," she warned, cutting Holly's protest off before she could make it. Instead, Holly stood and grabbed the rest of the plates, oddly flattered that Cathy wanted to spend this time with her.

In the kitchen, Cathy stopped at the sink. She set the dishes down before leaning forward to gaze out the window that overlooked the backyard. As Holly approached, she could see father and son, standing at the edge of the wheelchair ramp. Ross was pointing at the small, flowering tree as Luke nodded.

"I'm just so happy you're here," Cathy said, grabbing the plates from Holly's hands and adding them to the pile. Holly's eyes widened in surprise. She didn't think she'd ever received such a warm reception.

"It's such a relief to see him happy. My Lucas has always been serious. And I've been worried about him. Always takes the weight of the world on his shoulders. My little Atlas, I used to call him. Still do, just not to his face anymore," Cathy said with a wink. "I'm glad that he's smiling again." Cathy's warm fingers found Holly's and she gave her hand a quick squeeze. "And I'm glad he found you."

The warm, maternal gesture stunned Holly into immobility.

"How long have the two of you been dating?" Cathy asked.

"Oh, uh. We're not really…we're not very far into things. We only met a few weeks ago."

"Really?" Cathy looked surprised. "Well, I'm relieved Luke hasn't been hiding you from us. But you two seem so comfortable together, so in sync, that I just assumed you'd known each other for longer."

She wasn't wrong. Holly had been pleasantly surprised at just how much they had in common. The drive down had been a blast. Easy conversation, lots of laughs, they'd even established some inside jokes. If she wasn't lying outright to his face and he wasn't the prime suspect in the betting scandal she was investigating, then hey, they might actually have a future together.

The joke sobered her. Luke was a really great guy. He was completely devoted to his family, who were totally worth it, as far as she'd seen. He was confident without being cocky, serious without being stodgy and despite his intense image, he was still able to relax and make her laugh. The sex was pretty incredible, too.

He was the total package. And, she reminded herself, innocent until proven guilty, despite her suspicions. So really, *she* was the problem in this relationship. Fortnight of fun. Spring fling. Whatever you wanted to call it, she was the only verified liar in their midst.

And for what? For a job? But it was more than a job. And not just because the story she was investigating was career making. She was actually starting to come around to the Women's Hockey Network stuff. It was kind of fun.

And she'd gotten a few really nice emails forwarded to her from the Portland Storm site that said stuff like, "You saved my marriage," or, "I get why my boyfriend is into this stuff now," or just, "Your show makes us laugh." It made her feel good to know that this wasn't just three months of career limbo. She was getting exposure and she was touching people's lives.

And she was sitting on a sports scandal that would propel her into the big leagues. Especially now that Corey Baniuk's old job was up for grabs. Besides, she and Luke hadn't agreed to anything. They weren't even dating. Like the Women's Hockey Network, their time together was temporary, and it would be lunacy to put her future in the hands of a man she was having a tryst with, no matter how skilled and sexy those hands might be.

Holly glanced at him through the kitchen window.

Especially since Luke didn't trust her. And with the evidence mounting, she couldn't quite trust him, either.

The sound of rattling dishes pulled Holly back to the present, and she was surprised to find that Luke's mom had completely finished loading the dishwasher while Holly had done little more than stare starry-eyed out the window at her son.

"There, all done," Cathy said, pushing the door to the machine closed and wiping her hands on the tea towel she'd plucked off the counter. "Can I tell you again how much I love your show?"

"Aw, thank you, Cathy. That means a lot. Especially since I would imagine you know everything there is to know about hockey, whether you like it or not."

Luke's mom grinned. "I am a bit of an expert. Job hazard of being the mom of two sports-obsessed boys. I thought Luke might be the most hockey-crazed kid ever, but along came Ethan, every bit as hockey crazy. That child came out of the womb ready to outdo his older brother at anything he possibly could."

She folded the red-and-white checkered towel into perfect thirds and hung it on the oven door.

"For a while, Ross and I used to worry that it would impact their relationship. But Lucas…he's just got a special temperament, I guess. They've been thick as thieves their whole lives, until…well. We've all struggled since

Ethan's accident. But I hope one day that we'll find our way back. I catch glimpses of it sometimes, when Ethan forgets to be angry. My boy's still in there."

Holly's eyes stung, but she did her best to hold back the tears. Cathy's words were not for her—they were the words of a mother who'd come to the aching realization that her son's happiness was out of her control and it was a fact that she resented the hell out of. Holly had never missed her own mother more than she did right then, witnessing the strength and the heartache in Cathy's face, the duality of maternal love.

The Maguire men were a very lucky bunch.

Wiping her eyes, Cathy made a shooing motion with her other hand. "Oh, listen to me. We old people are always going off on tangents! I will not waste this beautiful day blathering when I could be learning all about you. I'm going to make us a pot of tea, and we're going to go enjoy some girl chat out on the deck."

LUKE FOLLOWED HIS dad around the backyard, taking in his latest updates. The old man had done a lot of work. Installed wheelchair ramps to make both the front and back doors accessible, widened all the sidewalks and his car was parked outside because he'd revamped the garage into a physio studio for Ethan. As they stopped to admire the apple tree, Luke could hear the muffled banging of weights behind the door.

Luke glanced at his dad. "How's he doing?"

Ross Maguire shook his head. "He's still so angry. But determined. He's in there every day, does his exercises religiously. Everything that made him such a great hockey player—the focus, the drive—he pours into his recovery. The physiotherapist is astounded by his progress, but Ethan has a hard time accepting praise because he's not where he wants to be. I don't know how to break it to him that he might never be."

The pain on his father's face was unbearable.

"I've never had to do that before, Luke. I've raised two extraordinary men who've accomplished everything they've put their minds to. No one's explained the protocol for when dreams don't come true."

"You're doing fine, Dad. Better than fine. Look at this place. You remortgaged the house to make every inch of it accessible. Ethan's gone to the best doctors, the best rehab clinics. His physiotherapist is practically part of the family, she's here so much. And as much as it sucks, there's nothing more we can do. The rest is up to Ethan."

Ross Maguire nodded. "I know you're right, son. But it doesn't make standing on the sidelines any easier."

Luke raked a hand through his hair. He hated himself just then, because even as he bore witness to his father's hurt, Luke had the overwhelming urge to yell, "No one's asking you to be on the sidelines of *my* life! I'm your son, too. I got named captain, my team made the play-offs and I'm struggling, playing worse than I ever have. And you haven't asked me about a single one of those things! I'm not even sure you watch my games on TV."

But he couldn't say any of those things without being a completely selfish bastard, so instead, Luke said, "I'm going to see if Ethan needs a spotter for his workout," and then he headed toward the garage.

"Got room for one more?" he asked as he entered.

Ethan barely glanced up at the intrusion. He was on the lat pull-down machine, doing heavy weights and high reps. Luke watched the sweat drip from his brother's determined brow. He was going to hurt himself if he kept up this demented pace. And yet Luke respected the hell out of him for sticking to it. For believing.

Luke stepped between the parallel bars, the spot where Ethan had willed himself to walk again. First one step, then twenty, then a few more. In that moment, Luke had wanted to believe, too, that Ethan would one day be free of the wheelchair. But after that, his brother's progress had stalled. And with each passing day it became less and less likely that he would ever fully recover. Ethan refused to accept that. But as Luke had learned as the captain of the Portland Storm, somebody had to be the voice of reason.

He understood that his parents couldn't bring themselves to dash the hopes of their little boy. And that meant that Luke would have to raise the possibility.

Stalling, he anchored a hand on each of the waist-high bars. He pushed up until his feet left the floor and his arms were straight. Then he launched into a quick round of tricep dips, pounding them out until his arms started to burn a little.

The clank of weights dropping let Luke know that he had an audience. He swung his feet back and forth a few times before dropping to the ground.

"What do you want, Luke?"

"I was hoping if my boys win this afternoon, that maybe you could attend the sledge hockey state championships with the team for me. If our series against Montana goes well, I'll be out of town."

Ethan was shaking his head before Luke had even finished speaking. "I can't. I'm training."

"You're always training, E."

"If I can't walk, I can't skate. I need to keep working. I can't afford to lose focus now."

Luke watched as Ethan pulled the pin and raised the knee pad on the lat machine. Slowly, carefully, he pushed himself into a standing position. He waited a moment, hand on the machine, to make sure he was stable. Then he backed up a step, then another, then another.

"No one's more determined than you. I know that better than anyone."

It was all Luke could do not to rush over and help him, to push the wheelchair closer, to swear at the injustice that had left this young, virile kid with the walking skills of a decrepit eighty-year-old man.

But he didn't.

Ethan made it, slowly but surely, back to his chair.

"You might be four years younger than me, Ethan, but you've always been right on my heels. Anything I ever did, you did faster and better, including hockey. And I know you miss it. But it's been three years since the accident. Three intense years, and you've been training nonstop."

Now Ethan did look up at him, and Luke could read betrayal in his brother's eyes. "You don't think I can do it? You don't believe I'll skate again?"

"I have no doubt that you will accomplish all kinds of great things in your lifetime, Ethan. You've always done anything you put your mind to. But I'm wondering at what price. As powerful as your single-minded focus is… We're just worried about you, little brother. Mom, Dad, me. You're in here for hours every day. You're only twenty-two years old. I don't want life to pass you by."

Ethan's laugh was bitter. "And what kind of life do

you think is passing me by, Luke? I spent a whole year barely able to take a piss by myself. People have to open the door for me. I can't drive. I can barely reach the damn stove. Physio is the only thing that makes me feel even halfway normal. Working out is the only thing that's helped me get better."

His voice broke. Ethan swiped at his cheek, erasing any sign of weakness. "And I fought through it. I fought through the pain and I won. I went from not being able to stand, to being able to walk five steps and then ten. It's measurable. I can see myself improving and I need that. Because that's what's going to make my life better."

Ethan shook his head. "That hit took everything from me, Luke. It took my body. It took my career. It took my dream. You can't understand what that's like because you're still playing. You're in the goddamn play-offs!"

"And I hate every minute of it! I can't concentrate, I can't score. Because I wish you were there instead of me."

"You want me to feel sorry for you? You want me to give up? Well, I won't. I'll do whatever it takes to walk again." His brother said the words like a vow.

"You're right," Luke said quietly. "This isn't about me. I want you to walk again, Ethan. I do. But I also want you to have a life. To enjoy yourself sometimes. To smile again."

"I'll smile when I can get rid of the chair and the crutches."

Luke scrubbed a hand down his face. "It's been three years."

His brother flinched like he'd punched him.

"Nobody wants to say it, but what if this is it, Ethan? What if this is as good as it gets?"

"Get out."

"C'mon, man. I just—"

"Stop treating me like I'm one of your damn charity cases, Luke. What are you even doing out here? Jesus Christ! Don't you understand? If this doesn't work out, I've got nothing!"

Luke shook his head at the injustice of that. "That's not true."

"Spare me the platitudes and get the fuck out."

With a sigh, Luke walked over to the door. He stepped outside and pulled the door closed behind him, but he hesitated to walk away.

There was a long pause, but then he heard the clank of metal that meant Ethan had resumed his workout. Luke headed back to the house.

He couldn't wait to find Holly and hit the road.

"You ready to go?"

Holly could tell something was on Luke's mind. He'd been distant since he'd come back to the house. Reading the signs, she'd packed up her suitcase and brought it down to the kitchen, anticipating his need for a speedy exit after his shower. She glanced over to where he stood, making jeans and a sledge hockey sweatshirt look good.

"Just about," she responded. "I wanted to say goodbye to Ethan before we go."

Luke tugged nervously at the brim of his black cap, and she could tell he wasn't wild about the idea. Neither were his parents, if their identical deer-in-headlights expressions were any indication. Little did they know, that was exactly the reason she was doing it.

She grabbed the bag she'd purposely left out of her luggage and headed for the back door.

With a deep breath for courage, she walked down the lovingly crafted wheelchair ramp and knocked on the garage door before stepping inside.

"Hi, Ethan. I hope I'm not intruding. My niece, Melissa, is your biggest fan and when she found out I was coming here, she asked me to see if you'd sign her jersey."

He'd looked pissed when she'd first walked in, but now there was only surprise in his eyes as she pulled the Team USA jersey from the bag, complete with "Maguire" and a big number ten on the back.

Ethan rolled his chair from the modified bicep curl machine he'd been using and approached her. He hesitated before he took the marker she held in his direction and even longer before he took the jersey itself.

"No idea why she'd want this," he muttered, scribbling his signature on the crest on the front.

"Are you kidding? You're her favorite player. Your goal in the gold medal game is what made her want to play hockey."

"That was a long time ago." Ethan clicked the lid back onto the Sharpie.

"Not so long," Holly countered. "People still remember. Just like they remember the dirty, after-the-whistle hit that took it all away."

Ethan's head snapped up at her bluntness.

"What happened to you was awful, completely unfair. But you can't let it define you. You can't spend your life focused on what you've lost."

"Did Luke put you up to this?"

Holly shook her head. "Nope. This is all me."

"You're going to walk into my house and tell me how to live my life? Like I give a fuck what my brother's new girlfriend thinks of me?"

"Oh, I'm not Luke's girlfriend. We're just sleeping together."

The expression on Ethan's face was almost comical, but Holly didn't pause to enjoy it. She had too much to say. "I'm just an outside observer, a hockey lover, someone who was sitting with Melissa when you scored that golden goal—one that will grace highlight reels for the rest of time. I saw the way you inspired my niece to try something new and the way your memory still inspires her to be the best at something that she loves."

Holly took a seat on a nearby weight bench.

"Your family loves you. They want to help you through this. And they're devastated every time you turn your back on their help."

"Leave my family out of this!"

Holly ignored him. "Luke's in the longest scoring drought of his professional career. He's playing like shit in the play-offs and beating himself up over it every single second. All because he feels like he's letting you down. But he straps on those skates every day and tries to do better, because he holds on to the hope that you might be watching.

"It kills him a little bit more with every game that you're not in the stands to cheer him on, but he'd never tell you that. Just like he'd never tell you that he's got a number ten sticker plastered to the inside of his helmet."

Holly shook her head. Her eyes prickled with unshed tears, but they were for Luke, not for Ethan, so she didn't let them fall.

"You know, I wanted to play hockey my whole life,

but I wasn't any good. I washed out. I was a horrible skater and I couldn't keep up with the other kids, so I decided to pursue hockey in a way that I *was* good at. I changed my focus to something more realistic. I took up sports journalism and broadcasting and now I get to be close to the game I love.

"There are opportunities to be part of hockey that don't involve playing. Television stations would kill to have you as a commentator or an analyst. Hell, Luke would love your help with the sledge hockey foundation. But if you're not into that, there are hundreds of sports-related charities dying for big names to bring them some much-needed press and support. There are also a ton of hockey teams out there, from the underprivileged ones all the way to the pros, who need mentors, or assistants, or coaches. And all of them would consider it an honor to have you aboard."

Holly got up and walked over to stand in front of Ethan. "So I guess what I'm trying to say is, the only one who thinks you're stuck in that chair is you." She grabbed the jersey from his slackened hands and held it up. "Thanks for the autograph, by the way. My niece is going to love it."

AFTER WARM HUGS with his parents and a promise that she'd come back to visit soon, Holly and Luke and their luggage were back in his truck and headed for the arena.

The game was amazing. Holly had never watched sledge hockey before and she was in awe. The kids were strapped into their sleds and propelled themselves around the ice with what looked like elongated miniature hockey sticks in each hand. Luke did his best to commentate for her, explaining how the butt end of the sticks had little metal teeth that gripped the ice and how a flip of the wrist was all it took to go from shooting the puck to speeding down the ice.

The logistics of the game hardly mattered as the game progressed. These kids were playing their hearts out, loving every minute of it, and by the time the Millerville Sled Dogs vanquished their opponents 3–1, Holly was cheering as loudly as anyone in the arena.

She followed Luke down to the Sled Dogs's dressing room, and they stood outside the open door waiting for the coach's cue.

"Great job today, boys! So good, in fact, that somebody special wanted to stop by and congratulate you on your big win!"

From the moment Luke stepped into the dressing room, it was obvious the kids loved him. Holly stood just outside the door, watching as he high-fived everyone. She couldn't help but be impressed. These kids weren't excited to see a premier hockey player—this wasn't a hero-worship, get-an-autograph type of joy. The bond went deeper than that. They were excited to see an old friend.

"Luke! You came!"

"Of course I did. You guys think I'm gonna miss watching you play such a big game? Not for anything. And you were fantastic! You guys just made the state finals! That's a really big deal."

"Says the man in the middle of a play-off run."

Luke brushed off the comment, and Holly really admired the way he kept the focus on the kids. "I'm proud of you guys. You've worked so hard this season, and all the practices and the focus is paying off. You have a real shot at winning the state championship, and that's why I brought an extraspecial surprise guest to get you ready for all the media and interviews you guys are going to be doing! Please welcome Holly Evans!"

She waved as she stepped into the dressing room, laughing at the excitement and all the hoots and hollers that greeted the announcement.

For the next few hours, she and Luke had a blast filming the kids, asking silly questions and watching them emulate the interview styles of their favorite hockey stars.

Holly was so caught up in talking with the kids, taking photos and answering questions, that she didn't even notice when Luke slipped out of the room. She found him sitting alone at the top of the bleachers, hands in the pockets of his hoodie, staring out at the ice as the Zamboni circled slowly, erasing the game they'd just witnessed.

"Wow. Those kids really love you."

Luke shook his head modestly, but a flush crept up his neck. His embarrassment was so endearing Holly's insides went all squishy. "I get more out of it than they do."

"Oh yeah?" she asked, taking a seat next to him. The painted wood was cold through her jeans. "How do you figure?"

"It's just awesome to see their joy. Their genuine love of the game. Lots of guys lose that by the time they go pro. The people I play with, the people I play against, there's not too many who still love it the same way they did when they were kids. Too much bullshit creeps in. Contracts, ice time, money and constant criticism from the media, armchair athletes.

"But these kids are still pure. They still play for the love of the game. And when I see them happy, it just…"

"It just what?"

Luke shook his head. "Nothing. It's stupid."

She placed a hand on his shoulder. "Luke?"

He kept his eyes firmly on the ground for so long that she was sure he wasn't going to tell her. She squeezed his shoulder to let him know that was okay, but when she pulled her hand away, he met her gaze.

"It makes me hope that maybe, someday, Ethan will find a way to be happy again, too, y'know? Some of these kids have never been able to walk, and some of them were injured, like him. But this game, this team, it makes them smile, despite all the shitty stuff they've been through. I want that for my brother. Even for a second, I want him to remember that life can be good. That we can be good. Like we used to be."

Luke pulled his hands from his pockets, tugged on the brim of his cap and continued.

"Ethan was a superstar. One of those kids that you knew was destined for greatness. Scouts were sniffing around him by the time he was twelve, keeping track, asking questions. He was just so goddamn good that you couldn't help but notice him."

Luke shook his head. "At seventeen, my little brother scored the goal that won our country a gold medal. At eighteen, he got drafted first overall to the league. People had big hopes. And even though I was jealous as hell of the kid, at how it all came so easily for him, I was proud, too.

"Anyway, as fate would have it, he and I both ended up on the Wisconsin Blades that year—his first year as a professional hockey player. Because of our age gap, we'd never officially played hockey together. Some pickup at the local rink, ball hockey in the driveway, sure, but we'd never had matching jerseys, or been on the same line. And it was awesome."

Luke laughed, and Holly realized that he'd left her. He was back in that moment, reacting to some inside joke she couldn't hear.

"Seriously, I loved every second of that season, him down the center, me on the left wing. We dominated. The Blades breezed through the regular season and right into the play-offs. We thought nothing could stop us. That championship had our name on it."

He was wringing his hands together, picking at his thumbnail, bouncing his heel on the concrete beneath his foot. Agitation that would have warned her the story was about to take a turn for the worse, had she not already known.

"And then we hit the fifth game of the second round. We were up three-one in the series, winning two-nothing in the second period. The whistle blew and I headed for the bench. Then there was this thud behind me, and it sounded like every fan in the building gasped, as if they'd all gotten punched in the stomach at the same time."

There were tears in his eyes now, and he bent over, elbows on his knees. And she knew that for him, just telling the story was a punch in the gut.

"Everyone in the Blades bench was standing up, craning to see what had happened. And when I turned, there was my little brother sprawled out on his stomach on the ice, not moving at all. Still. Deathly still. I dropped my stick and gloves and moved. I don't think I've ever skated so fast or so slowly in my life.

"It took forever to get over there, and I was screaming his name. People grabbed me, held me back. I remember them yelling, 'Don't touch him! You can't move him!' but at the time, the words meant nothing. I just wanted to get to him. I just wanted him to wake up."

The tremble in his voice stole her breath.

"Then there were team doctors, and ambulance crews and spine boards. And they took him away, and there was absolutely nothing I could do to help him. He's my little brother, Holly. I was supposed to protect him!"

Luke scrubbed his hands over his face and she could feel his struggle to pull himself together. With a sigh, he sat straight and tall on the hard wooden bench, eyes still glassy with the old pain. She doubted he knew there were tears streaming down his face.

"It was the worst fucking moment of my life. And it haunts me every single day. It's always there. And it makes me feel like an asshole. Because if that's how it feels for me, I can't even imagine how much worse it is for him."

Holly knew the chain of events, of course. She'd watched the career-ending hit. And the aftermath. But hearing Luke tell his story, to actually see his pain, still so close to the surface, it made her heart bleed.

And all she could do in that moment, high in the dimly lit bleachers of the chilly, small-town arena, was put her head on his shoulder and cry with him.

11

HOLLY STOOD AT the counter of her father's kitchen, dicing onions, while Luke Maguire chopped peppers. It was like playing a surreal version of house, and Holly had to remind herself that the domesticity was just an illusion. After their trip to Millerville, they'd both wanted to continue seeing each other. But they agreed on very clear rules for their dalliance. Just sex, no commitments. Still, the lines kept getting blurred.

Like how he'd dropped her off at home at four o'clock, and by six she was on her way to his place, with only a quick stop to drop off her niece's newly signed Team USA jersey to slow her down.

Like how she'd spent the next two days at his fancy condo with him, having sex and watching movies and eating takeout.

Or how it had taken everything she had to keep her standing Tuesday night dinner date with her father and leave Luke behind. But when she told Luke why she was leaving, he'd volunteered to come with her.

Things were getting very complicated.

"Do you know what I enjoy about this?" He gestured back and forth between them with the knife.

Holly raised an eyebrow. "About the fact that I have boobs and you don't? I could take a wild guess."

Luke winced with annoyance. He was so easy to bait. "No. And keep your voice down. We're at your dad's house."

He was *adorable*, she decided. "Yeah, but he's not here," Holly reminded him, glancing at her watch. 6:20. He always ate at 6:30 on the dot. *Where on earth is he?*

"Besides," she added, "what else am I supposed to guess with you waving that blade around at chest height?"

"I was gesturing to signify us." He lowered his voice. "Our illicit affair."

"What do you like about us?" she asked, ignoring the way her heart stuttered at the topic.

"That we don't talk hockey."

She hoped her face didn't give away her disappointment at that answer. "Oh?" She turned back to the onions, dumping them into the pan on the stove. They sizzled as they hit the hot oil, releasing their fragrance almost immediately.

"Everyone in my life wants to talk about hockey. About Ethan. About the Storm. My thoughts on our last game. My thoughts on our next game. My thoughts on games I'm not even part of. Sometimes it feels like I don't talk about anything else. It's actually kind of a relief that you don't care about it."

Holly added the peppers Luke had cut to the pan, as well as the bag of stir-fry veggies she'd left in her dad's fridge last week.

She knew he meant it as a good thing. He was trying

to say he was comfortable with her, and it was a lovely sentiment. But it made her gut hurt. Because that thing that he liked about her? It wasn't her at all. She was dying to debate hockey with him. Ask him his thoughts on all those things he was tired of talking about and share hers.

She gave the veggies a halfhearted stir, forcing a smile when he stepped up behind her and kissed her neck. "I'm glad," she lied.

And it reminded her that their entire relationship was based on lie after lie. Luke might be comfortable with this woman who didn't exist, but it was Holly's real heart on the line.

There was a big commotion at the front door and while it was right on time, it was much too big to be *just* her father.

Holly groaned inwardly. Her brother and niece must've decided to come over for stir-fry. Karen was probably working a stretch of nights at the hospital, and Neil was a notoriously lazy cook when his wife wasn't around to supervise.

Holly's suspicion was confirmed a moment later when a hungry eight-year-old girl came rushing into the kitchen. "Smells good, Auntie. Dad and I were going to have McDonald's but…" Melissa trailed off, eyes round as hockey pucks as she started to hyperventilate. "You're Luke Maguire. Ohmygosh, you're Luke Maguire!" By the end of the sentence, Melissa's voice was so high-pitched only dogs could hear her.

Holly laughed. "Breathe, monkey."

"Dad, Luke Maguire is at Grandpa's house! Are you staying for dinner, Mr. Maguire?"

Luke nodded. "That's the plan."

"That is so awesome! Your brother is my favorite player of all time. No offense."

"None taken," Luke assured her.

"Aunt Holly got my Team USA jersey signed by him. How cool is that?"

"She did?" Luke's raised brow held questions she didn't want to answer.

"Luke, will you sign my hat? Aunt Holly, is there a marker around here so I can get my hat signed?"

Saved by the autograph seeker. Holly rooted through the junk drawer as Melissa flitted around like a butterfly drunk on excitement. "My team's in the play-offs, too, you know. Just like yours."

"Is that so?"

"Yep. And we're gonna win, too. Dad! Luke Maguire is in Grandpa's kitchen. He's gonna sign my hat. Dad?" Melissa disappeared back into the living room in search of Neil.

Thank you, she mouthed at Luke, tossing him the marker she'd found. He caught it easily, but he waved off her appreciation like it was no big deal. Considering he'd finished explaining to her how much he'd been enjoying his hockey reprieve, she found his kindness toward her niece even more touching.

"So that's why you went to see Ethan before we left. Why didn't you tell me?"

"Oh, you know," she said, nudging the drawer shut with her hip. "I was worried your fragile ego might not be able to handle that Melissa's heart belongs to your brother."

Luke made a halfhearted effort at a laugh, but his preoccupation was obvious. "He actually signed it, though?"

"Yeah. He signed it."

The relief on Luke's face was heartbreaking.

"I'm really sorry about all this craziness. I understand that you were trying to escape hockey. I didn't realize it was going to be a full house."

Whatever Luke was about to say was cut off as Melissa marched back into the kitchen, pulling her dad along by the wrist.

"Nice try, monkey. You expect me to believe a hockey superstar is hanging out in Grandpa's kitchen and…"

"Told you." Melissa pulled off her ball cap and handed it to the hockey superstar hanging out in the kitchen.

Holly suppressed a laugh as her brother lost all ability to speak. His complexion, every bit as fair as her own, flamed red as he recognized their guest.

"Neil, meet Luke. Luke, this is my older brother, Neil."

"Hi. Wow. Hi."

Luke grinned as he signed Melissa's hat and handed it back to her. "Nice to meet you, Neil."

"You, too. Wow. Just…wow. Why didn't you warn me, Hols?"

"Or me," added her father. "When you said you were bringing someone home for dinner, this was definitely not who I was expecting," her father said gruffly, extending a hand. "Frank Evans. It's a pleasure to have you in my home."

Luke shifted the marker to his left hand so he could return the handshake. "Thank you for having me, sir."

"Okay, dinner's almost ready. How about everyone who just got home goes and washes their hands so they can help set the table."

"The table?" her father scoffed. "The first game of

the Buffalo-Wisconsin series is on TV right now and you want us to eat at the table?"

Holly shook her head in defeat. "Why do I even bother?"

TEN MINUTES LATER, Holly was sitting on the couch, sandwiched between Luke and her brother, with Melissa on the floor at Luke's feet. Pop, as always, was comfortably ensconced in his recliner. All of them were enjoying heaping bowls of teriyaki chicken stir-fry.

The first period featured some pretty intense hockey, and her family was in fine form, heckling the refs and players alike, hypothesizing the trades they'd make if they ruled the hockey world.

"Hey, Luke?"

He grinned down at the star-struck girl at his feet, and Holly hated her traitorous heart for noticing how good he was with her.

"Hey, Melissa?"

"Um, remember the time you scored that goal against the Wyoming Stallions back on October seventeenth? You stole the puck from Alfredsson at the blue line and then you skated so fast and scored right through the five-hole? And the goalie was just lying there 'cause he couldn't even believe it?"

Luke chuckled at the description. "I have a vague memory of that, yes."

"I was at that game," Melissa told him. "It was awesome. Aunt Holly took me for my birthday."

Oh my God. As if her "I don't speak hockey" cover wasn't tenuous enough *before* the last few hours. Now a witness had placed her at the scene of the crime. Holly jumped to her feet. "Okay. I think that's enough hockey talk for today. Who wants dessert?"

The answer was a unanimous yes. When Luke tried to help her gather up the supper dishes, she shook her head firmly. "I got it," she said, hurrying into the kitchen.

Thankfully, her family was too caught up in the on-ice battle to notice Holly's odd behavior. Luke, however, followed her into the kitchen before she'd even finished unwrapping the store-bought brownies.

"You sure you're okay? You seem a little distracted tonight."

She reached into the cupboard to grab a stack of napkins. "It's fine." She tried to smile. "I just feel badly for you. You were saying earlier how nice it was not to talk hockey every moment."

"Sure, but that?" He thumbed in the direction of the living room. "That brings back memories. Yelling at the television, armchair coaching and that instant connection you can have, even with a stranger, as long as he's wearing the same jersey as you. I'd forgotten how great the game could be from this side of the boards. It's a lot different than watching game tape."

Holly was touched by his kindness. He was trying to fit in and put her family at ease.

He stepped closer to her and his hands came to rest on the small of her back. "But somehow, I don't actually believe that's the reason you're so distant tonight."

"Oh no? What, are you a mind reader now?" she joked, resting her hands on his chest.

"Maybe I am. Are you thinking of the number... four?"

She shook her head, not understanding. "Four?"

"It's numerology," he said. Holly had to forcibly remind herself to breathe during the pause that followed. "If you add up all the letters in Vancouver, you get four. Not nine, like you said. Not nine, like Jay's birthday. Four."

Uh-oh. That was not an auspicious start to the conversation. Dread seeped through her stomach lining, and the stir-fry soured in her belly. "You've known for that long?"

"I did the math that night, when I got home."

Busted. On the bright side, it was probably the nicest way she'd ever been called a liar.

"I told you the day we met that I was on to you. Hockey is not a sport for the weakhearted. You're either all in, or all out. And I had a hunch you were all in. But now... I just wanted you to know that I know. You don't have to pretend with me anymore. Okay?"

Holly nodded. "Yeah. Better than okay."

He leaned in and the kiss was sweet and filled with relief. It was nice to be assured that she didn't have to hide that part of her around him anymore. That some part of what they had was based in truth.

"Great. So let's go watch some hockey." He grabbed the plastic tray of brownies and stack of napkins she'd set on the counter.

Her phone rang, and she recognized the name of one of her freelance clients, *Sports Nation*, on the caller ID. "Right behind you. I just have to take this first."

"More brownies for me, I guess," Luke joked, heading back into the living room.

She was smiling when she answered the phone.

"Holly? It's John Marshall from *Sports Nation*."

"Hey, John." That was odd. He was the senior editor

at one of the biggest blogs she wrote for. Except for the day he'd called to offer her the freelance job, he usually stuck to email, and even then his messages tended to come through lackeys. "I'm just waiting for the final buzzer so I can finish up tonight's game wrap-up. Should have it to you within the hour."

"That's great, Holly, but it's not why I'm calling. I actually wanted to talk to you about publishing one of your op-ed pieces."

Holly's heart revved, thudding against her rib cage. "I'm sorry, what?"

"Don't play coy with me," John joked. "Every second week, you submit an article about something going on in the world of sports and beg me for a byline. I'm finally going to give you what you want."

"Oh my God! John, that's amazing. Seriously. I couldn't be happier." Holly was practically bouncing. This was a big deal. She couldn't wait to tell her dad.

"Which article finally convinced you? The one about the evolution of goaltending equipment? No, it's my analysis on the new hybrid icing rule, isn't it?"

"Actually, it's neither. Those were solid pieces, but I could publish them any time, interchangeably. There's no *oomph* to them. The one that really impressed me is not only provocative and well-argued but incredibly timely. It's the perfect storm of sports articles."

"Don't leave me in suspense! Which article are you…"

Oh no. Holly's shoulders hunched even as all her muscles braced for bad news. *He doesn't mean…*

"How Luke Maguire Is Hurting His Team."

Holly's stomach bottomed out.

"It's fantastic, Holly. Obviously, I'll have to update it a bit since you wrote it at the beginning of the play-offs—his scoreless streak has hit sixteen games now—but all in all, it's got huge potential for our site. If it does as well as I think it will, who knows? I'm always on the lookout for insightful staff writers."

The line between dream and nightmare blurred. She'd been sending in articles for two years without a word from John, and the minute she got hired by the Portland Storm, the minute she and Luke were, well, whatever they were, *this* happened? She'd written that article two months ago. Before the Women's Hockey Network had even existed.

"You can't publish it, John."

"Yes, I can, Holly. The submission guidelines clearly state that once you send it in, I own it. And I will publish this article—"

She didn't have time for legalese right now. "Fine. Publish it, but I need you to pull my name off it."

"What are you talking about? You've been begging me for a byline since the day I hired you."

"John. The article is yours, but no names, okay?"

"I guess we can go with Anonymous. Might give the article more legs if everyone is speculating about who wrote it."

Great.

"You're sure about this, Holly? *Sports Nation* is a major player. Being published with us tends to help careers."

Holly's fingers migrated subconsciously to her lips. Lips that had just kissed the mouth of a man she cared for more deeply than she'd ever expected to. There was no choice.

"I'm sure."

STANDING OUTSIDE THE Storm's dressing room with the puck set to drop in about two hours, Holly knew she'd made the right decision.

She'd been concerned about Luke, first and foremost. She hadn't even thought about this job in the moment. That meant something. Something big. Something much too complicated to dissect right now.

But as she stood with Jay and the rest of the scrum, waiting for pregame access to the dressing room, she realized she was having fun. Sometime in the last month, she'd come to really enjoy this joke network of hers. Publishing with another company would have voided this contract, and she wasn't quite ready to do that.

The doors finally opened, and she stood back, letting the rest of the reporters head in. She had a good relationship with all the players on the team now, so she never wanted for interviews. Even the big names would carve out a little time to tell her whether they preferred dogs or cats.

She was just about to head in, when Brett Sillinger pushed through everyone in his quest to leave the dressing room in a hurry. His brow was creased and his scraggly play-off beard did little to hide his frown and the determined set of his jaw. The phone in his hand was blaring the "Charge" rally.

That damn anthem had become her nemesis. Every time she heard it—which in the course of a day's worth of interviews with twenty-three players on the active roster, was a lot—her heartbeat tripled and she went on high alert. She couldn't help herself. Even though she knew it was a clue with a lot of dead ends, it remained the most concrete lead she had.

If she could just re-create that bathroom happenstance, overhear the right conversation at the right moment, she'd have her man. She'd lost her chance for a byline on that damning article she'd written because she didn't want to hurt Luke, but the silver lining was the fact that she hadn't blown her cover with the Storm. Now she was *this* close to an on-camera exposé on a betting scandal. It was the kind of hard news story her mom would have killed for. The kind of legit sports reporting that might impress her dad.

That was why, with a quick apology to Jay and directions on a few questions he should ask should the opportunity arise, Holly hurried after the rookie. His long strides had given him a pretty good head start.

When he disappeared around a corner at the end of the hallway, Holly took a quick moment to stop and take off her pumps. Television shows that portrayed their women detectives chasing down perps while wearing high-heeled boots were such a load of crap, she decided. She resumed her chase, more sure-footed and quiet with her shoes safely in hand.

The hallway came to a T intersection, and Holly stopped for a second, debating which way to go. She decided any direction was better than no direction. She arbitrarily went left. When she got to the end of that hallway, she came to a skidding halt outside the occupied room, not at all prepared for what she found.

J.C. had his hands up to protect his face, ducking and covering as his fiancée screamed and swung her fancy designer purse like a flail.

"I can't believe you did this!"

Whack.

"I can't believe you would do this to me! To the baby! How am I supposed to show my face with the other hockey wives?" *Whack.* "Why would you sell the Porsche? Who's going to take us seriously driving some low-end four-door!"

"Come on, Tania. Quit hitting me with your purse already!"

"I'm going to be a laughingstock."

Holly tore her attention from the fighting couple, backing away slowly, trying to leave unnoticed.

She almost made it, too, but Tania gave a particularly wild swing of her bag, and J.C.'s gaze caught hers. She didn't even break stride. She just spun and ran.

Cowardly? Maybe, but she was hot on the trail of a suspect, and Tania's brand of a woman scorned was more than she cared to deal with right now.

Obviously, Sillinger had gone in the opposite direction, so she hurried back to where she'd lost him and turned the other way.

She was relieved that it did not take long to locate his nasally whine.

"What the hell, man? I thought we had a deal! I told you, I just need a little more time!"

Holly stopped short at the outburst. Her scalp prickled at the realization that this might be the break she'd been searching for. She tried to recall the harsh whisper that had echoed off the tiles in the Storm's bathroom. Had it been the rookie all along?

"Dude, you can't do this to me. I'll get you your money. Just give me a week. Two, tops. My mom'll help me out. She's in Vegas on vacation or I'd have your cash right now."

Holly frowned and leaned forward to peek around the corner.

Brett shoved a hand in his dark curls, his knuckles

white, he was clutching his hair so tightly. He pressed his back against the concrete wall, then slid down until he was sitting on the rubber floor.

"You don't understand. The Lamborghini's all I've got. My teammates think I'm a joke. This is the only thing I've ever done to impress them. Just give me a couple of weeks. I'll get you your money."

There was a long moment of silence, followed by, "Yeah. I understand you've got a business to run. Whatever."

He swore, then slammed his phone on the ground before wrapping his arms around his legs and dropping his forehead to his knees. All in all, it was quite a dramatic show.

"Brett?"

He started like she'd hit him with a cattle prod. He scrambled to his feet. The pout on his face made him seem even younger than his nineteen years, despite the pitiful beard.

"How long have you been there, Holly? What did you hear?"

Holly shook her head and started toward him slowly with her hand out, like she was approaching a skittish deer. "I just wanted to make sure you're okay."

"No, Holly. Actually, I'm not okay. I just found out they're repossessing my Lamborghini, so life pretty much sucks balls right now."

She did her best not to laugh.

After such an intensely emotional weekend with Luke, his parents, Ethan...the idea that a nineteen-year-old hockey player making a salary that most people could only dream of, herself included, was pouting like a child because he couldn't make the payments on his Lamborghini seemed the height of absurdity to her. Talk about your first-world problems.

She stared at the simpering man-child before her and mentally crossed his name off the suspect list. A man raking in extra money by betting on his team wouldn't have to ask for money from his mother. Even more damning was Brett's complete inability to deal with surprises.

Point-shaving was a delicate balance, especially in a low-scoring game like hockey. The idea that the kid before her had the chops to handle and manipulate a rink full of veteran hockey players was ridiculous. Truthfully, she was a little embarrassed she'd put him on the suspect list at all.

"You're not gonna tell the team, are you? About my Lambo getting repossessed?"

"No. I'm not going to tell them about your *Lambo*," she said dully.

"Okay, great. Maybe I can make up a story about how I totaled it or something. That would make me sound cool."

Holly let Brett disappear around the corner so she wouldn't have to walk back to the dressing room with him. Then she put her high heels on again to slow her down even further.

The dressing room was packed. She sidled up to Jay as soon as she spotted him. "What'd I miss?"

He shook his head. "No idea where J.C. is. I scored some face time with Eric and Doug, asked them the stuff you wanted for the 'How Well Do You Know Your Teammate?' segment. We're up next with Luke, after Baniuk finishes with him."

Holly watched Corey and his cameraman set up the shot and launch right into the interview.

"I'm Corey Baniuk from *Portland News Now*. Here with me is the Storm's captain, Luke Maguire. Luke, *Sports Nation* has recently published an article saying that your play, in particular, might be suffering because it's your first time in the play-offs since your brother, former Wisconsin center Ethan Maguire, took a brutal hit in the post-season three years ago. What do you have to say to those allegations?"

Shit.

Holly had hoped she'd have a chance to warn Luke before the article hit the media. John must have pressed "publish" the moment he got off the phone with her.

Why hadn't she said something to Luke after dinner? On their way home? After they'd made love? Because she was a coward, that's why. And she'd wanted to enjoy what she had with him as long as possible.

The color drained from Luke's face for a split second before it returned with a vengeance. "No comment. We're done." He pushed past the camera and headed for the exit.

Holly hurried after him, but instead of the hunt she'd endured with Brett, she found Luke pacing in the hallway right outside the dressing room door.

She couldn't keep the concern from her voice. "Are you okay?"

"I just need a minute."

"I saw what just happened with Corey Baniuk, Luke. You don't have to be fine. He coldcocked you. That was way out of line."

Luke just shrugged. "Rumor has it Baniuk's about to inherit the anchor desk. I should have expected him to go for the jugular on that interview, go out in a blaze of glory."

He took a breath. "Besides, Baniuk's not the problem. He was just the first reporter to get a crack at me. The problem is the damn *Sports Nation* article." Luke shook his head. "It's going to dredge up all the Ethan questions again. That guy really hit me where I live."

He lowered his voice, leaned toward her, and Holly could only hope he couldn't smell the culpability rolling off her in waves.

Luke continued. "The article talks about how my scoring drought started on the same day the team was mathematically guaranteed a play-off spot. This guy just laid out all my neuroses. I don't even get how he could figure out half that stuff. Much as it hurts to admit it, it's a really professional and well-written article. No cheap shots, just facts.

"It's probably for the best he didn't have the balls to sign his name to the thing. I'm not sure if I should pay him for the therapy or punch him in the face."

Luke shook out his hands. He was moving around a lot.

Holly, on the other hand, was frozen to the spot under a blizzard of remorse and shame. How had she thought taking her name off the article would ease the impact? She should have fought harder to keep it from being published in the first place. Again, coward.

Luke didn't seem to notice her anxiety. "Anyway, the article doesn't matter. What matters is that I've got a game tonight and I need to calm down and get back in the zone."

He drew in a deep breath and exhaled slowly. "We really have to win tonight. Any advice?"

She couldn't make her confession now. That would only screw with his head more. As the cause of his messed-up equilibrium, the least she could do for him now was to keep quiet.

Holly tucked her hair behind her right ear as she stepped toward him. "Montana's notoriously weak on their left side, so just keep the pressure on. Forecheck hard and whenever you get a shot on Krouse, remember to shoot stick-side. His glove has been hot in the post-season."

Luke grinned at the counsel. "Man. You weren't kidding when you said you know hockey."

"Kick the Wolfpack's ass tonight and I'll show you what else I know," she teased. It was a desperate attempt to keep the guilt from winning.

It didn't work.

12

IT WAS PAST midnight by the time Luke finished doing press and they'd arrived back at his place. Still, when Luke walked out of his ensuite bathroom wearing nothing but black sweatpants, Holly's weariness dissipated at the prospect of making good on her promise. Luke had kept up his end of the bargain and the Storm had come out victorious, downing Montana 5–3.

"So, what have you got in store for me tonight?" he asked, joining her on the bed. "And bear in mind that you're going to have to pull out all the stops to impress me, since I am currently a man in possession of flavored body oils and a tin of Altoids."

"Oooh! Flavored oils? Sounds fun! Where are you stashing 'em?" Holly rolled onto her stomach and reached for the bottom drawer of the nightstand closest to her.

"No! Not that one!" Luke practically vaulted over her, pulling open the small top drawer instead.

Holly shot him a frown. "What? Is that your fetish drawer, or something? You don't want me to find your ball gag?"

Oh my God, is Luke blushing? Her curiosity bubbled to new heights.

"It's nothing, okay? You wanted sexy oil, here it is." He pulled the lube out and set it on the end table. "Ooh, look! Cherry flavored."

"Nice try." She couldn't keep the grin from her face. "What's in there, Luke?"

He shrugged but it looked painful, like his skin was too small for his body. "Remember how we were going to have sex? Remember that fun plan?"

"But how am I supposed to really concentrate on doing naughty things to your body when all I'll be able to focus on is what's in that drawer?"

"You are very bad at taking no for an answer, do you realize that?"

Holly shook her head and heaved an innocent shrug. "What can I say? Our misogynistic culture has forced me to become a fighter, to believe in my dreams and power through the glass ceiling. You're part of the patriarchy, the reason I must pursue things with such single-minded determination. Face it, Mags. You're fighting a losing battle here."

With weary defeat on his face, Luke flopped back onto the bed and slung an arm across his face. "Fine. But you cannot, upon pain of death and/or laryngitis whenever there's a camera on you, tell anyone what you've seen here today."

Holly smiled graciously in victory. "What is it? What is it?" she chanted, pulling open the drawer. "What the...?" To her utter amazement, she found a pair of knitting needles attached to what she assumed was a striped scarf. But as she began to pull, the haphazardness of the striping became obvious, as did the never-ending length. "Seriously, what is it?"

Luke heaved a long-suffering sigh. "I told you. It's nothing."

Holly was still searching for the end of the navy, white and teal monstrosity. It was at least twice as long as she was tall and she still hadn't pulled it all from its resting place yet. "It's a pretty long nothing."

"It's just knitting, okay? My mom taught me."

Holly sat on the edge of the bed, yanking foot after foot of inconsistent stripes into her lap. "Okay, you have got to tell me how this came about."

Luke pulled his arm away from his face and stacked a pillow under his head. "When I was young, I used to really dwell on stuff—especially hockey games. If we lost, I'd go over it again and again, trying to figure out what I did wrong, what I could do better. If we won, I'd try to deconstruct what went right, how I could build on it. I was a pretty intense kid, especially once my little brother started climbing the hockey ranks. I'd get so deep in my head that I developed some pretty bad insomnia."

Holly ran her hand across the yarn in her lap. She could imagine a young Luke, solemn blue eyes, a determined set to his chin as he figured out how to be faster, stronger and better, all in the name of the sport he adored. He was still doing it.

"So she taught me how to knit. She said knitting would keep the chattering part of my brain occupied so I could mull over only the most important stuff and keep my thoughts really focused. She made the rule that I could only go over the game until I was done knitting five inches and then I had to put the yarn away."

He smiled. "It sounds dumb, but it worked. I would replay the game for however long it took me to knit five inches, and then I was free. I didn't have to think about it anymore. I've made one of these every hockey season since."

She held up the project in her hands. "All color-coded to your team, I hope."

Luke laughed at himself. "Yep. For my Portland Storm years, navy is a loss, white is a win and teal is a tie. Every game is five inches of knitting or purling and intense contemplation."

"So it's a good thing that this is mostly white then, huh?"

"Yeah, it was a pretty good season."

"And these thin teal lines at this end? That's the start of each play-off series?"

He nodded. "No ties in the play-offs, so that's my way of keeping track of how far we make it."

"You are a very surprising man, Luke Maguire. Just when I think I've figured you out, you change the game. Although I'm pissed at you that you told me that your secret talent was speaking French. This is way cooler."

Luke rolled his eyes.

"I'm serious," she said, with a playful punch to his arm. "I just have one more question."

"Of *course* you do."

"How do you hide it from the other guys on road trips?"

Luke grinned. "Nobody ever thinks your World Junior Championship duffel bag is full of yarn."

"Hiding in plain sight." Holly laughed. "Well done."

She set the knitted record of the Storm's current season on the end table. Every piece of himself that

Luke revealed made Holly fall in love with him just a little bit more.

How could she hurt someone she loved? And she would hurt him; that seemed inevitable. But was it better to hide the truth from him and let him have his win? Or come clean and destroy everything? There were no easy answers. She only knew that she wanted him to be happy, and tonight she could make him happy.

"I gotta say, that knitting was a much sexier find than a ball gag."

"Oh yeah?"

Holly nodded. "Yep. And now that my curiosity is sated, I find myself with plenty of naughty things percolating in my brain."

"You don't say."

"I *do* say," she countered, crawling over and straddling him. She grabbed the end of his knitting project. "So here's the plan. We're about to take your knitting to a whole new level."

LUKE LAY BACK against the pillows as she tied up one of his wrists before looping the free end of the yarn monstrosity through the slatted headboard. His body was already approving where she was going with this, even before she'd finished fashioning the woolen shackle around his other wrist.

Although his restraints could easily be slipped with a few tugs, her foray into light bondage was turning him on in a big way. He loved the satisfaction in her smile as she surveyed him, all trussed up and at her disposal.

If he'd known knitting would score him this kind of action, he would have opened the damn drawer himself.

"So now what?" he asked, unable to hide the desire that was tenting his pants.

"Now," she said with a wicked grin, "we get to the naughty stuff."

"I was hoping you'd say that."

She leaned down and kissed him with a brute force he hadn't expected. But he liked this take-charge side of her, the way her tongue plunged into his mouth, the bite of her nails on his chest.

When she pulled back, the look on her face undid him. She was this incredible mix of sweetheart and vixen, and the sugar-and-spice combo was proving to be never-ending fun.

She maintained eye contact as she stood on the mattress, stripping off her jacket, then her skirt. His breath came faster at the sight of her curves, highlighted by a purple bra and matching panties.

She dropped to her knees, then crawled forward between his legs. "Your turn."

Luke couldn't help the groan that escaped as she grabbed his pants and tugged them slowly down his legs. The torturous rasp of the elastic waistband against his hard flesh culminated in a harsh gasp when his erection was finally freed of its confines.

She tossed his pants to the floor and then stretched to grab the cherry lube. He loved her body, loved watching her move. She was a real woman, not a skeleton with boobs, and when he got free from his knitted prison, he was going to do some exploring of his own.

The lid on the oil tube opened with a soft *click*, and the intent look of concentration on Holly's face as she drizzled cool liquid on his hot flesh made his hips buck.

Dropping the recapped bottle on the mattress, she

reached for his straining cock. But then she jerked her hand back. "Wait!"

"What?" The word came out harsher than he meant it to.

"Can we jump right into this, or do you need to knit first?" she asked. The fact that she would stop to tease him just then made him want her even more.

"Only if you can't come up with a better way to get my mind off the game and tire me out."

Her smile said she had some ideas that he just might enjoy.

He was not disappointed. She wrapped her hand around his cock and pumped once, twice, three times to ensure an even distribution of the oil.

Then she put her hands on the bed beside his hips and took him in her mouth. His whole world shrank to the warm, wet pressure of her lips and her magical, magical tongue.

"Mmm."

The vibration of her sound sent another level of pleasure humming through his veins, and he flexed his hips, seeking more but unsure how things could get any better.

She lifted her head, releasing him from her mouth after a hard suck of his crown. "The cherries taste good, but next time, I'd rather just taste you," she said. Then she grasped his cock firmly in her right hand and proceeded to push him farther toward oblivion.

He was dying to bury his fingers in her soft, blond curls and set her pace, but he was also loving the torture of being restrained. The soft, suctioning sounds of her mouth were his undoing.

"Holly, I need inside you. I want to make you feel as good as I do right now."

He slipped his hands free of the yarn shackles so he could reach for her, pull her up the bed, taste her lips and move her body beneath his.

She sighed as he drove into her, slow and deliberate, but it didn't take long until he gave in to the roar of his blood and sped his pace. Holly didn't seem to mind. She drew her knees up, hooking her legs around his waist. The change in position forced him even deeper, and she started chanting his name against his lips.

He gave her everything she wanted, following her whispered orders until her breath grew choppy and her fingernails dug into his back.

Then Luke redoubled his efforts, plunging harder, faster, deeper, until he felt her body clench. And then he let her cries of ecstasy pull him over the edge right along with her.

SHE WOKE UP to find the bed empty. But the curtains blowing in the warm Portland breeze solved the mystery of Luke's whereabouts before she even had a moment to be curious. With a sleepy smile, she stretched and slid out of the bed. As she was grabbing her shirt, a familiar mix of navy, white and teal caught her eye. She padded across the hardwood floor to the chair in the corner of the room.

No way was Luke getting away with this blatant show of hubris without a goodly amount of teasing. She pulled the jersey on and headed toward the balcony.

Luke stood on the balcony wearing nothing but a pair of low-slung jeans, staring contemplatively out at the city. He looked so damn yummy that certain parts of her anatomy perked up at just the sight of him.

Down, girl.

"Seriously, Maguire. You have your own jersey in replica? That is so wrong."

He glanced over at the sound of her voice, and she could tell she'd surprised him. His jaw flexed as he took in the jersey, her thighs, calves, bare feet. His eyes tracked every inch of her and when their gazes met, there was an appealing cockiness to his expression.

"No, what's wrong is how much it's turning me on that you're wearing it. I like seeing my name on you."

"How very Neanderthal," she joked, walking over to him.

"What can I say? Me horny, you hot."

She laughed as Luke stepped behind her, placing one hand on the railing on either side of her hips. With a contented sigh, she leaned back against his chest. They stared out at the city as the sun came up over Portland.

It was romantic, standing in his arms and watching the world wake up. But after awhile, Holly couldn't silence the niggling voice in her brain, the one that said Luke was not the type of guy to indulge in blatant self-worship, and she turned in his arms to face him.

"So seriously, why do you have your own jersey? And why is the number wrong? Misprint?"

Luke shook his head. "No. It's not a misprint. It was for Ethan. I bought it for him after they gave me the *C*. I thought maybe he'd come to a game or something."

Holly's heart went a little melty. She traced a finger down his bare chest, hoping he'd say more.

Luke tightened his grip on the balcony railing. It took a moment, but he finally spoke.

"He's the reason I'm the captain now. Because I have to play for both of us. It was just my way of saying thanks. But you saw him. He's been so down, I just didn't have the heart to give it to him."

Holly suddenly realized the significance of the twenty-eight on the back of the jersey. Forget melty, her heart was liquid goo, sliding down the inside of her rib cage. "Eighteen plus ten. You added both of your jersey numbers together."

Luke shrugged, as if it wasn't the sweetest thing she'd ever heard.

"Like I said, it was dumb. It's been sitting on that chair for three months now."

"I'm sorry I put it on. I didn't realize it was so significant. I was just giving you a hard time."

"You know what? Keep it. No one else is going to wear it."

Holly had plans to the contrary, but she kept those to herself. "You're sure you don't mind?"

"Why would I mind? You look sexy as hell in it."

She smiled at that. "Well, if that's what you think about me in it," she teased, ducking under his arm and heading for the door, "then you should see me out of it." Luke followed her back to bed and she proceeded to prove her point.

AFTER ANOTHER HARD-FOUGHT win at home, they'd split away games in Montana, losing the first and winning tonight. And while Luke was glad they'd managed a win, he found he owed more of his good mood to the prospect of seeing Holly again than to the game result. Luke loosened his tie and looked out the oval window at the lights of whatever city they were currently flying over.

"Mags, you okay?"

Luke glanced over as J.C. took the aisle seat beside him.

"You're staring off into nothing. I thought you'd had a stroke or something."

"How did you know Tania was the one?"

J.C. laughed. "What?"

"I'm serious, man. You two are getting married, having a baby. How did you know she was the one you wanted to do all that with?"

Normally the stymied expression on his goaltender's face would have made him laugh, but tonight he just wanted answers.

"Where is this coming from? Wait a minute, are you dating someone?"

Luke took a deep breath. He wasn't really ready to spread the news around. He certainly didn't want to put Holly's job at risk. But he was dying to tell someone, and J.C. was his best friend. He couldn't help his smile when he said her name. "Holly."

"Holly? As in, *Holly* Holly? Of Women's Hockey Network fame? The woman you don't trust because she is undermining the sanctity of the game and threatening the team? *That* Holly?"

Luke accepted the ribbing as par for the course, but when he didn't fire back, J.C. sobered a little. "You're serious? You have feelings for this girl."

Luke shrugged, which in guy talk was as good as a yes.

"Huh. Never took you for the kind of guy who'd end up with a ditz just because she's got a nice rack."

Luke's shoulders stiffened. "That's over the line, man." His voice was all steel, and J.C. held his hands up in a gesture of surrender.

"My bad, man. Just testing the waters. I wasn't expecting to come back from the can and have you start talking about your emotions and shit. Stand down."

Luke relaxed in his chair, but not until he'd stared J.C. down, let him know he meant what he said. "And for the record, she's not a ditz. She just plays one on the internet."

"Whad'ya mean?"

"The dumb blonde routine is all an act. She's actually as smart as she is beautiful." He sent his buddy a sidelong glance. "And she knows more about hockey than you ever will."

"So then what's with all the secrecy?"

Luke shrugged. "I guess the top brass doesn't think we're good enough actors to answer the questions if we thought she was only joking."

"Ha. They believe us well enough when we line up to kiss their asses at all their hoity-toity events."

Luke smiled at the dig. Everyone was aware of how much J.C. hated putting on a tux and schmoozing with the bigwigs.

"So what's Holly's deal then?" his friend asked. "She's like, a reporter or something?"

"She wants to be."

J.C. nodded. "Cool. Good for her. And good for the two of you. I'm happy for you guys. Truth is, Mags, the fact that you're asking me how you know? That probably means you already know." J.C pushed the button that made his seat recline. "I'm gonna catch twenty minutes before we land."

"'Night." The word came out distracted, though, as Luke let the words settle in.

That probably means you already know.

13

THE GAME WAS going well until the hit. The sight of Eric Jacobs lying on the ice and clutching his knee was too much.

With a feral growl, Luke dropped his stick and his gloves and launched himself at six feet, two hundred pounds worth of smug left-winger. He grabbed a fistful of Wolfpack jersey with his left hand and landed a solid hook with his right. He only had a second to relish the roar of the crowd and the sting in his knuckles before his punching bag recovered and launched a counterattack.

But Luke wasn't about to back down. He might not have gotten the chance to punish the man who put Ethan in a wheelchair, but he wasn't going to let the one who'd just sidelined Eric Jacobs get away with it unscathed.

Despite Chris Powell's attempts to wrestle him into submission, Luke managed to land a few more good blows to the jerk's face before the two of them overbalanced and fell to the ice. Luke swore when his nose made contact with Powell's helmet, his eyes welling up at the sharp sting.

He didn't have time to worry about it, as he struggled to gain the upper hand even as someone grabbed him by the shoulders and pulled him back.

"That's enough, you two. Break it up." The ref's voice managed to penetrate the angry haze that had overtaken Luke's brain, but he was too worked up to obey.

With a final jab to Powell's left cheek, he let himself be hauled off the asshole who'd just lambasted Eric Jacobs with a dirty, knee-on-knee hit.

He watched his nemesis scramble to his feet, only to be detained by the referee.

"Nice fight, Powell," he taunted, ignoring the linesman's attempts to wrestle him over to the penalty box. "I think you might have even broken a nail trying to hug me into submission."

"You should thank me for not messin' up your face there, pretty boy. Might lose your 'hottie of the month' status and then you'd have to play hockey for a living. How many games has it been since you last scored?"

The idea that he and Powell had been linemates a mere four months ago, before the other man's giant ego and philandering ways had sent the bastard to Montana, seemed ludicrous in that moment. Obviously things changed. Loyalties faded. You couldn't trust just anybody.

"Tell your boys I said good luck in the play-offs, Maguire. It's gonna be a battle without your top scorer."

Luke followed Powell's gaze toward the net, where Cubs was being helped off the ice by the trainer. Luke didn't like the way his centerman was hunched over, his left leg bearing no weight.

The ref skated up. "Shut your mouth and get moving, Powell." Then he turned to Luke and gave him a shove. "That goes for you, too."

The other linesman skated up, handing Luke his stick and gloves. The memories that came flooding back were not happy ones, and even though Eric's injury wasn't as serious as the one that was haunting him, it was cold comfort.

With a sigh, Luke headed for the penalty box. He'd gotten two minutes for instigating and five for fighting. Powell got two minors and a game misconduct.

The Storm ended up winning the game and the series with it, but Luke barely made it through the post-game press junket. By the time he and Holly got to his place, his palms were clammy and he couldn't stop shaking.

Everything with Ethan had been so close to the surface lately. To see another talented player—another centerman, for God's sake—get taken down on Luke's shift…it made his heart feel too big for his rib cage, like it might puncture any second.

"I can't do this again."

"He's going to be okay, Luke. Here, just crawl into bed, okay?"

"But what if he's not? His grandma had a heart attack a few months ago. He needs to be able to take care of her."

"He can. He got off the ice himself. He's not as badly hurt as Ethan was. And even if he had been, there's nothing you could have done to stop it. It's not your fault." Her voice was soft. Reassuring. He liked hearing it. It made him feel better.

"I'm the captain. I'm responsible for my team."

"I know you are. But you couldn't have stopped this."

She crawled in beside him, and for the first time since the fight with Powell, he began to breathe normally.

"Maybe I could have. I should have tried. I should have done something."

"Luke. Stop. You did everything you could."

Holly wrapped her arms around him. His heart slowed to its standard pace.

"Will you stay tonight?" he asked.

"Sure, of course."

Her warm fingers stroked his hair. It wasn't too long after that, that Luke surrendered to sleep.

IT WAS SIX THIRTY in the morning when the sun streaming through Luke's window woke Holly. He was slung out on the mattress beside her, and she was glad to see him resting after his post-game panic attack. He'd been through so much lately. Too much. And there was more to come.

He shifted on the mattress, sliding his hand over her hip and tugging her closer. She turned to face him. His blue eyes blinked a few times before they opened for good. "Hi."

She smiled and ran a finger down his stubbly cheek. "Hi back."

"Sorry about last night."

"There's nothing to be sorry about."

Luke sighed. "Holly, I can recognize a panic attack when one hits. I had them really bad right after, well, right after Ethan got hurt. Last night wasn't anything compared to those ones, but I really appreciate you staying here and talking me down."

"It's not a problem, because..." she trailed off.

"Because?"

I love you. She did, but she couldn't say it yet, though, so she kissed him instead.

He kissed her back and shifted closer. Before she knew it, they were naked and entwined, his body driving into hers with such an elemental force that for the first time in their relationship, there was no need for sexy words, or woolen shackles, or flavored oils. They were beyond all that. And when her climax rolled in like soft tides instead of roaring waves, it was the most exquisite thing she'd ever experienced.

They were holding hands and trading kisses and indulging in a dreamy discussion about breakfast— he was firmly in camp bacon and eggs, while she was leaning more toward French toast—when the "Charge" anthem intruded on their blissful post-coital haze.

Luke rolled away from her so he could locate his phone, and the loss of his body heat sent a chill down her spine. It took him a few moments of searching— he'd been in such rough shape last night that most of his before-bed routines, like putting his phone on its charger, had been annexed by the panic attack.

She watched as he followed the familiar music toward the chair where she'd slung his suit jacket after she'd helped him take it off. He flipped the expensive fabric around so he could access the interior breast pocket. Finally he got hold of his ringing prey.

"H'lo? Yeah, it's me."

His whole body tensed, and Holly felt the distance he put between them even before Luke pulled on a pair of jeans. He didn't miss a beat on the phone that was expertly cradled between his ear and his shoulder.

"No way. I told you, that's not an option," he said, stalking out of the bedroom. "I don't care how you do it, just get him the money. I can't have this traced back to me."

The words stopped her heart. She jumped up with some half-formed plan to follow him, but she only made it three steps from the bed before the unthinkable caught her eye.

Dazed, she walked toward his jacket, askew on the chair back, just as he'd left it. A folded piece of yellow legal paper poked out of the inside breast pocket.

She unfolded it to find a list of letters and numbers in stark black ink.

And just like that, her perfect morning crumbled.

It can't be Luke.

The man who was so sweet and thoughtful, the man who needed hockey to breathe, surely he wouldn't do something that could earn him a lifetime ban from the game he loved?

And yet there were other things—his parents' modest dwelling and pile of bills, Ethan's intense physio regime and state-of-the-art equipment, the fact that a hockey player who should have adequate funds had said things like "money's tight" and "I can't have this traced back to me." Something wasn't quite adding up there. She'd tried her best to find a more viable suspect, but something always cleared them.

Brett Sillinger had pouted when his Lamborghini got repoed.

J.C. LaCroix had done the responsible thing and downgraded to a family car because he had a baby on the way.

And Eric Jacobs, who'd been her least likely suspect in the first place, had apparently been dealing with some intense family issues that correlated with his slightly-below-average play-off showing.

Luke, on the other hand…

Holly sat on the edge of the bed, the over/under list clenched in her fist.

He'd shown up in the bathroom moments after she'd found the betting sheet, and his ringtone matched the mystery man's.

His truck was nice, but in the grand scheme of luxury vehicles, it was pretty low on the scale for a six-year veteran who was currently earning almost two million a year.

His parents must've invested huge amounts of money into making their old house fully accessible, not to mention the cost of Ethan's physio studio and medical bills. And she'd heard several sports outlets reporting that Brad Timmons had recently filed for bankruptcy, which meant the Maguires were receiving no financial help from the man responsible for their money woes.

And she'd caught Luke twice now in the midst of suspicious-sounding phone calls, the most recent one specifically about untraceable money.

She didn't want to believe it. Luke loved the game and he was fiercely protective of his teammates. It was beyond comprehension that he would jeopardize his career or his team's integrity this way.

But even as she thought it, she knew there was one thing he loved more than hockey—his family. He would do whatever it took to take care of them. Manipulating the games a little was an easy way to help pay down his family's debts, to take care of his parents and his little brother.

And maybe that straight-arrow reputation he'd built

up—the one that made her doubt he was capable of it—
was the key to getting away with the crime. He had the
perfect cover.

She *had* to ask him.

She was in love with Luke and she owed him the
truth about her suspicions, the right to defend himself,
to give his side of the story. Before she exposed it to
the world.

14

"LUKE, CAN WE TALK?"

He'd barely stepped back into the bedroom after a massive fight with his brother's bank. The somber note in Holly's voice made the hair on his arms stand up. "Sure, yeah."

He took a seat on the corner of the bed opposite her. "What's going on, Holly? Is everything okay?"

"Yeah," she said, but she backtracked immediately. "No. It's not, actually." She sighed.

They made eye contact and he didn't like what he saw there.

"Luke, I'm just worried about you. I know you've had some money trouble."

"What?"

"You were obviously speaking with a bank just now. And I get it. Your family is amazing. And they needed your help, but manipulating hockey games...that's a dangerous road to start down. So if it's about money..."

His muscles tensed and his jaw hardened. This wasn't a talk. It was a cross-check after the whistle. The kind that left permanent damage.

"What are you trying to say?" His eyes dropped to the yellow paper clutched in her fingers. He shot to his feet, eyes lighting on his suit jacket, askew on the chair. "Have you been going through my things?"

"I found a list, Luke. When I was in the Storm bathroom that day that we kissed. This list. And aside from the first one, every single play-off game has ended with the same over/under as the list predicted. That's not a coincidence. Someone is manipulating the games."

"And you're accusing me?"

Her silence was all the answer he needed. Luke experienced a moment of full-body pins and needles and then…nothing. Numbness settled over him with a finality that reminded him of death. "You believe I would do that." It wasn't really a question, since she'd already said as much. More of a reckoning.

"Luke, I know how important your family is to you. You'd do anything it took to make sure they're okay."

He raked a hand through his hair. "But this? After all we've been through? I kept your secret! I introduced you to the people who mean the most to me in this world. I fell in love with you, Holly."

She looked like he'd punched her. That stricken reaction to the words he'd wanted to say for longer than he was willing to admit was the final nail in the relationship that had turned his world upside down. "And this is what you think of me."

Her brown eyes were swimming in unshed tears, and her chin trembled as she fought to hold them back. "Luke, the evidence—"

"Fuck the evidence! I would never do what you just accused me of! Not for any amount of money. I wouldn't do that to my family. I wouldn't do that to my guys.

We're a team, Holly. We trust each other. We back each other up. I can see you don't know anything about that, but that's how we operate. It's how we win games and it's how we lose games. Together."

"But the stats, and that phone call about untraceable money and Ethan's top-of-the-line rehab equipment…"

"That's your reasoning? Let me tell you something about money. Pro hockey players make around three hundred thousand dollars a year in the first three years of their contract. Unless they get paralyzed. Then they make nothing. But they still have to live, Holly. They need money to eat, to buy a wheelchair, to pay for medical bills and specialists and daily physio. Whatever it takes for the chance to walk again.

"The parents of an injured pro have to remortgage their house when they should be gearing up for retirement, because sidewalks have to be widened, ramps have to be built and garages have to be converted into rehab facilities. A paralyzed player needs a new van to accommodate a wheelchair. And when things start looking bleaker and bleaker, he has to figure out how to finance a car with hand controls so that a broken hockey player can live the fulfilling, independent life he deserves, even if he doesn't regain full use of his legs.

"So, yeah. Money's tight. My paycheck might have a few zeroes on the end of it right now, but there are millions of dollars of catching up to do. And the secrecy? The phone call you overheard? That was just for Ethan's pride. Because he's already struggling with accepting physical help, and I didn't want him to know about the financials, that the bastard who ruined his life claimed bankruptcy and that all his money is coming from me.

"He needs to focus on recovering, on himself, not

worrying about his family. And maybe I should have told him. But I'm his big brother and it's my job to protect him. I didn't do it on the ice that day, but I've damn well done whatever it takes to make up for it ever since. And that's my call. Not yours."

She was trembling now, and he hardened himself against her imploring eyes. "I'm sorry, Luke. I can see I made a mistake. I just wanted to bring my concerns to you. To be honest with you. And I realize this is hard to hear, but every prediction on the list I found has come true save one, and that is not coincidence. If it's not you, it's somebody else on the team."

His protectiveness roared up with a vengeance. "Leave my guys out of this!"

"I won't!" She came to her feet then, too, and the change in her, from meek acceptance of his lecture to formidable warrior ready for battle, was startling. "I sat here and I listened to your side. Just because you have an explanation for my evidence does not mean it was ridiculous, so don't you dare stand there and demean it. I'm an excellent reporter, Luke.

"I do my homework and I test my hypotheses. Just because my conclusion about you was proven false, doesn't let your team off the hook. This list still belongs to somebody who used the Storm bathroom that day." She held it up, and it trembled because her hand was also trembling.

"It's not mine, obviously," she said, "so by process of elimination, thanks to your ridiculous game-day superstitions, that means it's one of your teammates.

"And you want more honesty? You want to be able to trust me? You know that fair and honest article on the

Sports Nation blog? The one about how you're hurting your team? I wrote that."

Blood roared in his ears as he processed that betrayal.

"I wrote it before I ever met you and when I found out they were going to publish it against my objections, I asked them to take my name off it. Because not hurting your feelings and continuing to work for the Storm meant more to me than the byline that would have helped me reach my dream job in sports reporting.

"You think I'm out to hurt you and the team? Then why have I kept this illegal activity under the radar instead of selling the story to any number of media outlets who would pay me large sums of money and give me my pick of jobs? Your heart is not the only one that got bruised here. And while I've always admired your loyalty to your teammates, if you do not figure out who is poisoning your team right now, then you're all going to end up infected."

Luke crossed his arms, kept his voice level. "I think you've said everything there is to say. You should go."

"I agree." The tears she'd so valiantly held back spilled down her cheeks, but he refused to be moved. Holly's words were impassioned, but they didn't change anything.

All this time he'd been giving her his heart, and he meant nothing to her. Just as he'd accused her of from the start, all she'd wanted from him was a career-making story. She'd written the *Sports Nation* article. She'd been investigating them the whole time. And he'd taken her to his home. He felt sick to his stomach, like he'd just put the puck in his own net.

He'd let his heart overrule his head. Ignored the

clues—he'd caught her in her lies about not knowing hockey, listened raptly to her stories about her mother and her childhood dreams of becoming a reporter. She'd been rubbing it in his face for their entire relationship, and he was too stupid to have even noticed.

She might have kept this story secret for a couple days, but she wouldn't sit on it for long.

He should have trusted his instincts and fought harder to get her fired from the get-go. He'd had his own suspicions about the list but he'd let her distract him. And now his reputation, the reputation of his entire team, was going to be dragged through the mud in the court of public opinion. All because he couldn't keep his dick in his pants.

He was the worst kind of fool—a willing participant in his own downfall. That ended now.

"FIRED?"

The word felt like ash on her tongue, chalky and bitter. The taste of lost dreams.

"I'm sorry, Ms. Evans, but it was stated very clearly in your contract that you were not to interact with players outside of your professional capacity."

"But who—?"

"I'm sorry, but we can't release that information. Suffice it to say, a reputable source came forward and we have no choice but to enforce the terms that you yourself agreed to."

Said contract sat on Hastings's formidable oak desk, mocking her. Holly raised her eyes from the blinding whiteness of the paper with binding black type marching in perfect lines that reminded her the striped prison garb in old-timey movies. She raised her eyes to the man who sat across from her.

"I don't even get to defend myself?"

"I'm afraid the informant is a rather...important member of the Storm's organization."

Hastings was one hell of a finesser, she'd give him that.

"As such, we will be terminating your contract immediately and your services will no longer be required. In return for this short notice, you will receive your full compensation, as outlined in your notice of hire. Do you agree to these terms?"

"Do I have a choice?"

"I will take that as a yes." Hastings slid another piece of paper toward her. "We do require you to sign this nondisclosure agreement, which states that you will not discuss the details of this parting of ways, or anything leading up to it, upon threat of legal action."

She grabbed the pen and with numb fingers, scrawled her signature on the designated line.

Luke had sold her out. She'd gotten too close to hurting the team and he'd turned her in.

Betrayal burned white-hot in her chest, and she had to gulp to get enough air in her lungs. The fact that he hadn't even given her a heads-up... She understood that he was angry at her, but at least *she'd* had the courtesy to bring her concerns to him first, even though it had been the last thing she'd wanted to do. She'd been honest with him. To his face. Because she loved him.

She hated herself for it, but she did. Even when she'd believed he might have been involved in illegal activity, some part of her still believed that what they'd shared was real. And now, when he'd sold her out, she was still conflicted about breaking the story.

Luke had seemed genuinely hurt by her accusation, even as he'd confirmed all the reasons that some extra money could have gone a long way. She thought of Luke's parents, of Ethan, of everything the Maguires had been through. Luke loved his family enough to do anything for them, but she hadn't considered what a betting scandal would do to them if he'd been exposed. He would never have taken that risk.

She'd interpreted the evidence, but she'd boiled it all down to numbers, to probabilities and stats. She'd been so focused on doing what it took to get the job of her dreams that she'd failed to take the man himself into account. And now she'd lost everything. Her story. Her job. And the man she loved. Unsure what to do with herself, she gathered her things and headed for her father's house. He looked up with surprise as she entered the door.

"What are you doing here in the middle of the day?" he asked.

"I got fired, Pop."

"Oh."

"Oh? That's all you have to say about this?"

All her frustration, all her anger, everything she'd kept bottled up since the night she found out her mother was never coming home again roiled up from the depths and she was powerless to hold it in.

"Everything I've ever done is to make you proud, and you just look right past me!"

"That's not true."

"It is true! I've been sitting on this couch beside you for years trying to get your attention, and all you've ever done is ignore me and watch sports! So I watched sports, too. And I learned everything there was to learn about them. Players, rules, stats, just so we could have a conversation sometime. But you wouldn't even give me that! You just act like I'm not even here!"

"Holly—"

"Don't 'Holly' me! You talked sports with Neil! Why not me? Why not me, Pop?" She was too angry to cry, too exhausted to shout anymore. She was just empty. Holly sat on the couch in her usual spot and stared at the basketball game on the television.

"When I lost Mom, I didn't think anything could ever hurt as badly as that again. But I was wrong, because Mom didn't leave me on purpose. Not like you did."

Her dad got out of his chair and joined her on the couch. In her entire life, her father had never sat on the couch. She almost jumped when he put his hand on her knee.

"You remind me of her. Especially when you're on camera. That's always been hard for me."

Holly looked at her dad, felt like she was seeing him for the first time. "What?"

"You're smart and beautiful and you're so good at everything you do. Of course I'm proud of my girl. But sometimes it hurts to look at you because I miss her so much. I didn't realize how unfair I've been to you all these years. I never meant...I never meant to push you away. I love you, Holly. I do."

The words brought tears to her eyes. She couldn't remember the last time her father had said something nice about her, or told her he loved her. Throughout the years, his sporadic comments were always externally focused: "work harder, know more, do better." And she had. She'd lived her whole life striving to be good enough for him. To actually hear that he was proud of her made her heart swell.

"They were stupid to let you go. You're an expert at that game. If they can't see that, then they don't deserve you. And you'll show them. Because when you put your mind to something, there's nothing that can stand in your way. Now don't go and cry on me. I've never been good with that."

"Well, tough beans," Holly said with a watery laugh, and she hugged him. He stiffened in her grasp, but then his arms came around her and she felt his weathered hand pat her shoulder. It was like she was six years old again. Like she had her dad back. "I miss her, too," she confessed.

"She would've been proud of you. And she would have told you to fight for what you deserve. When life knocks you down, you get up and punch it in the gut."

His arms tightened around her, and she heard an unmistakable sniff.

"You okay?"

He cleared his throat and pulled away. "S'nothin'. Just got some dirt in my eye is all. Now you gonna stop yammerin' so we can watch the game, or what?"

Holly smiled as he got up and brushed his knuckles under his eyes. "Yeah. I'll stop yammering. How about I make us some popcorn to go with that game?"

He nodded gruffly as he dropped into his beat-up old recliner. "I could go for some popcorn."

15

"Paige! Open up! I need to talk to you."

Holly banged on the door again, this time with more force. Paige's phone had gone straight to voice mail—a regular occurrence, as her friend was notorious for forgetting to charge her phone. But Holly was desperate for counsel and she wasn't going to let a dead phone stand in her way.

"C'mon, Paige! I know you're in there. Your car's in the driveway. I really need your advice."

Finally, after what felt like a lifetime, Holly heard the snick of the lock give way. Paige's face appeared in the six-inch crack of the open door. "Holly, what are you doing here? Is everything okay?"

Holly shoved the door open all the way and barged past her friend. "*News Now* just called. They just gave me Corey Baniuk's old job. I'm the new roving sports reporter for the six and eleven o'clock news."

"Wow, Hols. That's fantastic! That's your dream job, right? Interviewing athletes on TV. That's everything you've been working toward."

Holly nodded, dropping onto Paige's couch—a sleek,

robin's-egg-blue torture device that was built for style, not comfort. "I know!" She glanced over her shoulder at her friend. "So why am I not happier about it?"

"Aw, sweetie." Paige rushed over, wrapping the lilac sheet tighter around her before she joined Holly on the couch. "What's going on?"

"I have no idea. This is everything I wanted! And since the Storm fired me, I should be doubly glad because it means I'm not unemployed, trying to scrape by on ghostwriting sports articles.

"I went for the interview this morning, and they offered me the position on the spot. But even as I was shaking hands and signing contracts, something felt... off, you know?"

Paige nodded reassuringly, readjusting her toga. All of a sudden, her new job wasn't the only thing that seemed off to Holly. "Wait a minute. Why are you wrapped in a sheet?" Holly stood. "And why did it take you so long to answer the door? Is someone here? Did I just catch you *in flagrante*?"

She walked back toward the door, cocking an eyebrow as Paige rushed after her, blocking Holly's path to the bedroom.

"Do you have a sex crush of your own? And is he, or is he not in this house right now? Do not lie to me, Paige Marie Hallett."

"What?" Paige's blush made her whole face blotchy, like she was allergic to the lie she was trying so desperately to formulate. "No, I was just... I mean I, I just..." Her eyes focused briefly on something to Holly's left before they darted back to the floor.

Holly glanced behind her. A familiar pair of worn Vans sat in the entranceway. "Those are Jay's shoes."

She whipped around to face her friend. "You're sleeping with Jay? You hate Jay! Since when are you sleeping with Jay?"

There was a long moment of silence, before a deep voice sounded from behind the door at the end of the hall. "Since she already knows, can I come out now?"

Paige sighed. "Yes. Come out."

The door to her friend's bedroom swung open, and Holly could barely process the sight of her barefooted cameraman wearing jeans and pulling his vintage Ghostbusters T-shirt over his head. His grin was sheepish as he ran a hand through his unruly brown hair. "Hey, Holly. Congrats on the new job."

The entire world had gone mad. Her dream job was making her miserable. Jay was sleeping with Paige. She was going to have to keep an eye on the sky when she left, because the odds of seeing pigs soaring over the clouds seemed pretty high right now.

"I need some water."

Holly headed into Paige's kitchen and grabbed a bottle of Evian from the fridge. She took a long swig of the cool liquid and followed it with a couple of deep breaths. "Okay, so you guys are sleeping together. I can deal with that. I'm an adult. Angry sex is a thing."

"Actually..." Jay slung an arm over Paige's shoulders. "We're kind of past the angry sex stage and on to the dating exclusively stage."

Holly knew he was telling the truth because Paige didn't slug him. Instead, her friend's bright green eyes turned imploring. "I'm sorry we kept it a secret, Hols, but we were trying to get a handle on it ourselves. I'm glad it's not a secret anymore, though, because you deserve to know. This never would have happened if not for you and the Women's Hockey Network."

"Say what now?"

Paige smiled at her. "You think the Women's Hockey Network was a joke, but the truth is you did great research and presented facts in a way that resonated with me. And with a bunch of people who aren't usually interested in sports. You gave us a foothold in a world we didn't understand. And not because we were incapable of understanding. You're not dumbing anything down. You're just coming at it from a different angle. Hockey got a whole lot more exciting for me when you snuck in a little medicine to the spoonful of sugar that is Luke Maguire's abs."

"Seriously, Paige? I'm right here," Jay lamented.

"Understanding the game made it more interesting to watch. Because of you, I suddenly understood offside, or why the whistle blew even though no one had touched the puck and why the face-off was happening somewhere other than at center ice. And that made me care more about the game."

Holly tried not to be touched, but to hear her sports-allergic best friend talking about offsides was kind of a big deal in her world. Damned if it didn't make her a bit misty-eyed.

"Basically, you made me realize what else I was missing out on. I mean, if hockey wasn't as bad as I thought, what else might be better than I gave it credit for?" Paige slipped an arm around Jay's waist. "Sometimes what you want doesn't look at all like what you thought you wanted. Nothing about Jay and I makes sense, but we just fit. And I owe it all to you because I might not have figured that out on my own."

"You think that dumb fluff is me at my most insightful? My mom is probably rolling over in her grave."

"I think she'd respect you for it as much as I do, Hols."

If she was being honest, at some point during this whole farce, the Women's Hockey Network *had* started to really matter to her. In her heart, Holly knew it was more than fluff, had known it for a long time.

It was just hard to reimagine her future, to reevaluate her priorities. She'd spent so long convinced that *real* sports reporting was her destiny. The only route to make her dad proud. The best way to honor her mother's legacy. But Paige was right, the only person who wasn't proud of her was herself.

"The thing that makes you great is that you care so much," Paige continued. "You're not supposed to be on *News Now* reading a teleprompter, you're supposed to be making real connections and improving people's lives." She remembered the little girl she'd met at the bakery. Paige was right. She *was* making a difference. Sometimes miniscule, like making people laugh, and sometimes major, like helping two people feel closer to one another. But either way, it was rewarding. It was still sports, still her passion, but it was so much more than that, too.

So she let go. All her expectations, all her goals, all her former dreams. Her chest felt light, as if her lungs were full of helium. Or freedom.

For the first time, Holly wasn't in someone else's shadow, or seeking someone else's approval. She knew exactly where her future lay and she had a phone call to make.

16

WAITING WAS A special kind of hell.

Every morning, Luke expected to wake up to an angry phone call from his agent and an even angrier headline in the paper. And every morning, there was nothing.

It was driving him crazy. He'd been sure it would have come by now. He'd worried about it through both of the Storm's out-of-town games, constantly monitoring the internet for any sign that Holly had broken her story. But she hadn't. Yet. The prospect loomed over his head like a guillotine.

And now they were back in Portland after two tough losses in Wyoming. They were hoping to even things out tonight with the home crowd behind them.

The tension in the dressing room was almost unbearable. His teammates were unusually quiet as they fidgeted in full equipment and waited for Coach Taggert to start his pregame speech. Instead, Taggert walked over to Luke, touched his shoulder pad. "Someone's here to see you."

Holly.

Her name popped unbidden into his heart. Was she here to apologize? Or to tell him she was going live with the story tonight? And why did the prospect of seeing her make his heart race with anticipation? He was mad at her. Furious, really.

"Now's not really the time, is it, Coach?"

The gruff, burly man motioned toward the door with a shake of his head. "You wanna stay a part of this team, you do what I say and trust me when I tell you, you wanna take this meeting."

Luke obeyed. But when he stepped out of the dressing room, it took a long moment before his brain could fully register the sight before him. "You came."

"Yeah, well. There's only so many places you can wear one of these jerseys, so…" Ethan shrugged.

Luke hadn't even noticed the damn jersey. The *C* on the front. The number twenty-eight visible on the sleeve. "Holly," he breathed.

His little brother nodded. "Yeah, it showed up in the mail the other day. Complete with a scathing letter that threatened me with bodily harm if I didn't get my ass out to one of your games. She's pretty incredible. Too good for you, really."

Luke couldn't even process the joke. "I'm glad you're here."

Ethan stared down at the ground. "I should have come before. It's been a really tough couple of years, Luke. Without hockey, I've got nothing. I've put everything into getting back on that ice, and every day it became clearer that wasn't going to happen, and I couldn't deal with that. But Holly helped me see that there are still opportunities to be part of hockey. Maybe not on the ice, but on the bench. Or in a studio. I can still talk about it, dissect it, coach it and watch my brother play it the way it's meant to be played." He looked up at that.

"You've always been in it for the love of the game. That's what makes you great, big brother. You do it for the right reasons. Not the fame or the fortune or the ladies. Because you genuinely love playing. You've got to stop giving a shit about my feelings, or what's going on with your teammates and just get out there and do what you do. And know that it's good enough, no matter what happens."

Growing up, he and Ethan had always been close, but the heartfelt words made Luke realize how much distance had crept between them since the accident. He'd been so busy trying to take care of things, he hadn't realized how much he'd missed his brother.

"Also, this is for you."

Ethan handed him a beat-up paper bag. Luke opened it and couldn't help but laugh. "No way!"

Ethan blushed as Luke held up a knitted replica of the Storm Jersey he wore, complete with "Maguire" and a big twenty-eight on the back and the coveted *C* on the front.

"You made this?"

"Yeah, well, I've had a lot of time to think lately. Had to break through some of that mental chatter. Figured if I was knitting, it might as well *be* something…not like your stupid thirty-foot lengths of nothing."

Luke shook his head. "You always gotta show me up, don't you, you prick?"

"It's not my fault I'm so much better than you at everything. Now got out there and win this game."

Ethan's words were still ringing in his ears as he stepped onto the ice. The game was going to be a battle. Down 2–0 in a series was not a great place to be, but for the first time since the play-offs began, Luke was in his element. He belonged there. Tonight, he was going to make sure everybody knew it.

A minute and twenty-seven seconds into the first period, Luke snapped his scoring drought with a beautiful wrist shot to the top-left corner.

IT WAS A hard-fought, physical game. Players from both teams spent their fair share of time in the penalty box, and despite the Storm's commanding first period, the Wyoming Stallions had battled back to a 3–3 draw with seven minutes left in the game.

Luke had thought they were destined for overtime, but with forty-six seconds left on the clock, the rookie redirected one of Kowalchuk's big booming slap shots, and the Storm had gone on to win it 4–3 in regular time. There was a tangible relief in the air as his weary teammates filed into the dressing room after the game. They'd held on, brought the series back to within one. Their dreams of the championship were still viable.

It took him a moment to notice that his goaltender was walking in front of him hunched over with the air of a man who'd just lost it all.

Luke grabbed his jersey, stopping him before he stepped into the dressing room with the rest of the team. "Hey man, you okay?"

J.C. barely looked at him as he shrugged. "Huh? Yeah, no. I'm fine. Good goal. You relaxed and played the game. Just like I told you to."

Luke frowned. "For a man who was just part of an epic, kick-ass win, you seem pretty down."

He shook his head. "It's nothing. Just tired. Play-offs are pretty grueling."

"Yeah, okay." Luke meant to drop it then, to give his goaltender—his friend—some space, but there was a niggling thought in his mind. A piece that wouldn't quite fit. J.C. wasn't acting like himself tonight. Hadn't been since… "You went down."

"What?"

"Third period. We were up 3–2. Johnson was coming in on his backhand and you went down. He scored top shelf. You never go down when Keith Johnson is on his backhand. You've been playing against him since we were fourteen."

"What are you talking about?"

"It's you." The realization vibrated in every cell in Luke's body. He stood facing his friend in the middle of the hallway, betrayal burning like lava in his veins. "Holly was right. You let that goal in on purpose. What the hell are you wrapped up in?"

For the first time, J.C. looked something other than listless. In fact, he looked downright panicked. He glanced around the hallway. "Would you keep your voice down?"

"What the fuck is going on?"

"Calm down. It's nothing." He put a comforting hand on Luke's shoulder.

Luke shook it off. "Are you betting on hockey? Are you betting on us?"

J.C. went from soothing to defensive in a split second. "What the hell's your problem, Mags? It's no big deal. It's over-under stuff. We've got a real chance this year. All I have to do is keep the score a little closer than it should be in a few games."

Luke's stomach churned with disgust. "I can't believe you! You could go to jail for this! You're about to get married. You've got a *baby* on the way."

J.C.'s face twisted with ire. "Why does everyone keep saying that like it's a good thing? Tania and I have been together for four years, and she wanted a ring or else. I didn't propose, I followed orders. And when the doubts took over, I was all set to tell her I wanted the damn ring back. But then she dropped the bombshell that I was going to be a dad."

J.C. ran a hand over his play-off beard and his voice turned beseeching. "A dad, Mags. Me. I'm too young to be a dad. I wanted to leave her, and now we're bonded together for the rest of time. And there's not a goddamn thing I can do about it. So I went to the track. A few times. Just to blow off some steam. And I got in a little over my head. But they offered me a way out—a way to clear up my debt. And we still win. Everybody wins. C'mon, man. We're the only ones left who know about this."

"What do you mean, the *only ones left*?" Realization dawned as soon as the words were out of Luke's mouth. "*You* got Holly fired? You son of a bitch! You used what I told you on the plane and you sold her out, you sold *me* out. I trusted you. I'm in love with this girl."

"She's a reporter, Mags."

"You're the one who insisted I was overreacting. That she was harmless."

"That was before I knew she was only pretending to be stupid! She heard Tania yelling about me getting rid of the Porsche. It was only a matter of time until she put it together. No one can find out about this. It wasn't personal, man. I was just covering my bases."

"J.C., what you're doing is illegal. You've put this whole team at risk. Jesus." Luke ran a hand through his hair. "What were you thinking?"

"I was thinking you had my back. Isn't that what you always say? Put the team first?"

Luke shook his head. He'd been so wrapped up in his guilt, so blinded by his insistence on protecting the team that he'd lost sight of what was important. "You think this is putting the team first? You crossed the line, man. You *deserted* your team, and as the captain, I can't let that stand."

"What, you're going to tell on me? Is that it, Luke? After all we've been through together, you're going to end our friendship and torpedo my career over a few goals that, in the grand scheme of things, don't even matter?"

Luke looked at his teammate, his friend, and saw a stranger staring back at him. "You're goddamn right I am."

17

"GOOD EVENING AND welcome to the eleven o'clock sports wrap-up. I'm Corey Baniuk and I'd like to introduce you to the newest addition to our team, Holly Evans. Usually, she'll be on the scene, covering games as they happen," he said. "But tonight we're happy to have her joining us in studio so that you, our viewers, can meet her properly. Holly, good to have you here."

"Thanks, Corey. And congratulations on your promotion." Holly smiled big and turned to the camera. "Hi, everyone. Let's start with hockey, where earlier tonight the captain of the Portland Storm, Luke Maguire, finally broke a nineteen-game scoreless streak with this beauty less than two minutes into their game against the Wyoming Stallions…"

Holly did the entire segment and it was incredible. She nailed the scores, the camera changes, every word that came out of her mouth was crisp and precise. It was a triumphant moment, but not quite as triumphant as the moment that followed it.

"Thank you, Holly. And now—"

"Actually, Corey, I'm not quite finished."

She'd never seen the golden voice of sports at a loss for words. Apparently it wasn't good for business, because the camera operators bobbled for a quick moment before every single one of them turned to focus on her.

"When I made the Women's Hockey Network video, I was being a smart-ass. I was frustrated that people would discount opinions on sports just because they came from a woman. So I created a satirical look at how women in the sports world are perceived.

"Except when my video hit YouTube, it went viral. The Portland Storm hired me for their play-off run, and everything changed. The Women's Hockey Network grew into something unstoppable, and I was just along for the ride. For a while, I thought I was making mockery of everything I loved. Then I heard from you, the people watching, and I realized that together, we had something special.

"I want to thank everyone at this station and you, the viewers, for welcoming me with open arms. This job was a childhood dream come true and I will remember this night for the rest of my life. But my priorities have changed, which is why tonight will be my only show with *News Now*. Effective immediately, I'm tendering my resignation.

"But if you liked the Women's Hockey Network, then I invite you to join me on XT Satellite Radio, where I will be hosting *The Women's Sport Network* every weekday from one to three on Sports Talk Radio. It's going to be a show where women can congregate and talk about sports. Where we can teach what we know, or learn what we need to know."

Holly could feel her smile warming as she spoke. "It's going to be real women asking real questions. If you don't understand the rules of the game, ask me. If you don't understand why the GM of your home team isn't moving on signing that free agent who lit up the field last year, we'll discuss it. And if you want to hear what cologne your favorite player wears, I'll find out for you.

"Because there are no stupid questions. I want to help every woman, every person, find the part of the game that appeals to him or her, because when it comes right down to it, sports are about having a good time. I lost sight of that for a while, but I finally found it again. And now I want to share it with you." Holly tucked her hair behind her right ear. "I'm Holly Evans, for *Portland News Now.* Thank you and good night."

Holly strode out of the studio without a single doubt that she'd made her mother proud. It was a great feeling, one she reveled in all the way to the lobby, until she glanced over at the security station and noticed a certain hockey highlight. She beelined toward the desk.

"Can you rewind that?" she asked.

The security guard grabbed a remote off the desk and turned to the monitor.

"Thanks, just run it back to the last goal that Wisconsin scored on the Storm. Yes. There."

Her skin prickled as she watched Keith Johnson walk in and score a top-shelf backhand on J.C. LaCroix, who was sprawled across the crease.

"Son of a—"

It all made sense now. The awful goal, the lackluster baby announcement, the vehicle downgrade and the purse-wielding psycho fiancée.

It had been J.C. she'd heard in the bathroom that day. He was the mole. She had to tell Luke! And if he wouldn't listen, well, she'd make him listen.

She'd just pulled out of the parking lot, formulating a plan to get Luke to let her explain herself when the radio announcer's voice penetrated her single focus.

"And we take you now live to a surprise press conference involving key members of the Portland Storm. We've confirmed that Captain Luke Maguire, Coach Randy Taggert and GM Ron Lougheed are all present, as is League Commissioner Grant McDavid. McDavid was seen during tonight's game sitting with former Blades centerman and national hero Ethan Maguire. Needless to say, the sports community is buzzing with speculation over what the big announcement is. We now go live to the Portland Dome."

Ethan had shown up?

Her grip tightened on the steering wheel, and she changed her course from Luke's apartment to the arena. But what could they possibly be talking about at a press conference? The post-game interviews had ended hours ago.

Holly shook her head. The biggest damn story of the day was unfolding while she'd been looking pretty on TV. And instead of sending her or Corey Baniuk, *Portland News Now* had probably sent some intern to cover it. Thank the hockey gods she'd quit.

"Thank you, everyone, for coming tonight. I'm afraid we're here with bad news."

Her stomach flipped at the sound of Luke's deep voice filling the airwaves.

"As the captain of this team, I would like to begin by saying the Storm organization has always prided itself on stressing the importance of sportsmanship and integrity. However, thanks to some incredible under-cover work by sports reporter Holly Evans, it has recently come to my attention that there is an individual on this team who has not been living up to the code that we, the Portland Storm, have sought to play by.

"This individual has been involved in betting, and when his debt got too big, he agreed to manipulate game results during our play-off run. As the captain of a phenomenal team, I have spoken with my teammates and we have decided, after consulting with the league, to withdraw from this year's play-off run and wish the Wyoming Stallions the best of luck as they take on the winner of the Eastern Conference."

The gasps in the auditorium were audible even through the radio, and Holly sped up as she approached the turnoff that would get her closer to the Portland Dome.

"We, as a team, in conjunction with our coach and management, feel this is the best way to keep one person's actions from tainting the entire team."

He knows. Oh God. She wondered how Luke was taking the devastating betrayal of his best friend's actions. His voice sounded even, if a little somber, but she'd need to look into his eyes to be sure.

"And with the league's support, we hope to earn our way back to next year's play-offs and claim our chance to win the championship.

"I personally would like to apologize to Holly Evans and thank her for her diligent work."

The car swerved a bit at that, as Holly tried to process the shock of Luke's very public words of praise.

"I love this game with all my heart and I could not have lived with myself if I had been part of sullying its good reputation, however unwittingly. The truth has come to light, and that's exactly how it should be. And for that reason, effective immediately, Jean-Claude LaCroix is no longer a member of the Portland Storm. Thank you. Coach Taggert will now say a few words."

Questions exploded throughout the press room, and Holly could hardly breathe as she pulled into the parking lot. She was relieved the attendant at the gate recognized her and let her through without a hassle, because she was having a hard time forming words.

Luke had done the right thing even though it had cost him his dream, and she wanted to throw up for doubting his integrity for even a split second. He'd not only taken the high road and given her credit for breaking the story, he'd even thanked her publicly. And for what? For jumping to conclusions about him? She had to get in there right away.

Holly screeched to a halt and parked in an illegal zone as close to the door as she could. She turned off the car, silencing Coach Taggert's "weathering this adversity will only make us a stronger hockey club" speech.

Then she ran—in heels—for the press room. By the time she got there, the league commissioner was handing down his ruling.

A security person stopped her. "Ma'am? I'm sorry, you can't go in there. Press only."

"I am press!"

"I'll need to see some identification."

Holly dug frantically through her purse until she came upon the lanyard she'd failed to return: her Women's Hockey Network press pass. And for the first time, her wide-eyed, helmet-haired photo wasn't an embarrassment, but a badge of honor.

The security guard let her through.

"Although there will be a further investigation by the league, the fact that the Portland Storm brought this breach of ethics to our attention immediately upon learning of it will go a long way in expediting the process. Mr. LaCroix has admitted to being the sole perpetrator and has been banned from the league indefinitely. At this time, we will be taking questions."

The room was a roar of sound as the scrum exploded with queries.

"One at a time, and please use the microphone."

As she approached the front of the room, the interrogation quieted, replaced with whispers as the gathered reporters began to recognize her.

She stopped in front of the microphone and Taggert nodded at her to proceed. "Holly Evans, from the Women's Sports Network. My question is for Luke Maguire."

The way he was looking at her broke her heart, part hopeful, part wary. It took everything she had to keep herself from running up on that stage and pulling him into her arms so she could apologize.

"Luke, I was just wondering, do you think there's any chance that you can forgive me? Because if you love me even half as much as I love you, then I think we could be a great team."

There was a long, silent moment where the world went still. Seconds ticked by to the beat of the pulse echoing in her ears.

A murmur spread through the crowd.

"Teammates, huh?" he said.

She nodded.

He leaned forward to speak into his mic. "I don't know."

Dread wound its way through her stomach and into her chest, squeezing her heart like a vise. She deserved this, she reminded herself. She'd known this was a possibility.

"You think you can handle that, Evans? Because if we do this again, I'm going to need you in it for the long haul, a hundred percent commitment. Eye on the prize."

Holly bit her lip as Luke got up from the table and pushed his way past the rest of the panel members. With every step that brought him closer, hope bubbled in her chest like a lava lamp. She was nodding before he even reached her. "I believe I can manage that, yes."

"I hope so, because I love you, too." When he pulled her into his arms, his kiss was everything—an apology, a declaration, a promise. Holly wound her arms around his neck, relief and love pounding through her veins in equal measure.

The room erupted in applause and camera flashes. But all that mattered to her was the man who held her in his arms. She was never going to let him go again.

"I thought I'd lost you," she whispered.

Luke smiled and it made her heart flutter. "Not possible."

"How do you figure?" she asked.

"You ever heard people say that love is a game?"

She nodded.

"When I play, I play to win. And just for the record, I expect my teammate to do the same."

Holly grinned and grabbed him by the tie. "Aye aye, captain," she said and sealed her promise with a kiss.

* * * * *

REQUEST YOUR FREE BOOKS!
2 FREE NOVELS PLUS 2 FREE GIFTS!

♦ HARLEQUIN®

Blaze

red-hot reads!

YES! Please send me 2 FREE Harlequin® Blaze® novels and my 2 FREE gifts (gifts are worth about $10). After receiving them, if I don't wish to receive any more books, I can return the shipping statement marked "cancel." If I don't cancel, I will receive 4 brand-new novels every month and be billed just $4.74 per book in the U.S. or $5.21 per book in Canada. That's a savings of at least 14% off the cover price. It's quite a bargain. Shipping and handling is just 50¢ per book in the U.S. and 75¢ per book in Canada.* I understand that accepting the 2 free books and gifts places me under no obligation to buy anything. I can always return a shipment and cancel at any time. Even if I never buy another book, the two free books and gifts are mine to keep forever.

150/350 HDN GH2D

Name	(PLEASE PRINT)	

Address		Apt. #

City	State/Prov.	Zip/Postal Code

Signature (if under 18, a parent or guardian must sign)

Mail to the **Reader Service:**
IN U.S.A.: P.O. Box 1867, Buffalo, NY 14240-1867
IN CANADA: P.O. Box 609, Fort Erie, Ontario L2A 5X3

Want to try two free books from another line?
Call 1-800-873-8635 or visit www.ReaderService.com.

* Terms and prices subject to change without notice. Prices do not include applicable taxes. Sales tax applicable in N.Y. Canadian residents will be charged applicable taxes. Offer not valid in Quebec. This offer is limited to one order per household. Not valid for current subscribers to Harlequin Blaze books. All orders subject to credit approval. Credit or debit balances in a customer's account(s) may be offset by any other outstanding balance owed by or to the customer. Please allow 4 to 6 weeks for delivery. Offer available while quantities last.

Your Privacy—The Reader Service is committed to protecting your privacy. Our Privacy Policy is available online at www.ReaderService.com or upon request from the Reader Service.

We make a portion of our mailing list available to reputable third parties that offer products we believe may interest you. If you prefer that we not exchange your name with third parties, or if you wish to clarify or modify your communication preferences, please visit us at www.ReaderService.com/consumerschoice or write to us at Reader Service Preference Service, P.O. Box 9062, Buffalo, NY 14240-9062. Include your complete name and address.

SPECIAL EXCERPT FROM

HARLEQUIN

Blaze

*Enjoy this sneak peek at A SEAL'S TOUCH
by New York Times bestselling
author **Tawny Weber**—a sexy, sizzling story in the
UNIFORMLY HOT! series from Harlequin Blaze!*

*Navy SEAL Taylor "The Wizard" Powell has a
reputation for getting out of tricky situations. Bad guys,
bombs—no problem. Finding a girlfriend in order to
evade matchmaking friends? Not so easy.*

Taylor Powell pulled his Harley into the driveway and cut
the engine.

Home.

He headed for the front door, located his key and
stepped inside.

"Yo," he called out as the door swung shut behind him.
"Ma?"

He heard a thump then a muffled bang.

"Ma?" His long legs ate up the stairs as he did a quick
mental review of his last CPR certification.

As he barreled past his childhood bedroom, he heard
another thump coming from the hall bathroom. This time
accompanied by cussing.

Very female, very unmotherly, cussing.

In a blink his tension dissipated.

He knew that cussing.

Grinning he sauntered down the hall. Stopping in the
bathroom door, he smiled in appreciation of the sweetly
curved rear end encased in worn denim.

The legs were about a mile long. The kind of legs that went beyond wrapping around a guy's waist.

He almost groaned when his eyes reached a pair of black leather boots similar to the ones he wore on duty. Was there anything sexier than legs like that in black boots?

"Hellooo," he murmured.

"What?" The hips moved, the back arched and the owner of those sexy legs lifted her head so fast he heard it hit something under the sink. Rubbing her head, the woman glared at him with enough heat to start a fire.

"Taylor?"

"Cat?" he said at the same time. He started to help her to her feet, but at the last second paused. Touching her so soon after that image of her legs wrapped around him didn't seem like a smart idea.

When the hell had Kitty Cat gotten hot?

Her golden hair was tied back, highlighting a face too strong to be called pretty. Eyes the color of the ocean at sunset stared back under sharply arched brows. The rounded cheeks and slight upper bite were familiar.

The way her faded green tee cupped her breasts was new, as was the sweetly gentle slide from breast to waist to hip where the tee met denim.

Oh, yeah. Kitty Cat was definitely hot.

"Hey there, Mr. Wizard," Cat greeted. "Still out saving the world?"

"As always. How about the Kitty Cat?"

"Same as ever," Cat said with a shrug that did interesting things to that T-shirt of hers.

Things he had no business noticing…

Don't miss A SEAL'S TOUCH by Tawny Weber, available February 2016!